FINDING J. HUBBARD

Elizabeth Young

PUBLISHED BY FASTPENCIL PUBLISHING

Finding J. Hubbard

First Edition

Print edition ISBN: 9781499906837

This book is entirely a work of fiction. No characters are intended to bear any resemblance to anyone alive or dead.

http://www.fastpencil.com

Printed in the United States of America

Table of Contents

PROLOGUE

Twelve years – could anybody still be looking for a body? Not likely, but possible. Of course, he had served his time. Would finding her now make any difference? Maybe to someone, but not clear who that would be. Still, always a little question in the back of the mind. Old mysteries fade away. This one should, too. Unless . . .unless . . .there might be someone. And supposing that person was successful? Then what?

CHAPTER ONE

Ellie's text made Zora's morning.

"Please come to dinner Sun. if you can. Just us." Zora accepted readily. She missed Ellie. When they lived in their next door Cambridge townhouses, they saw each other often, taking turns cooking or going out -- sometimes to Fenway Park for Red Sox games. Ellie's marriage to Tyler Sheppard changed all that – "as it should," Zora said firmly to herself. She looked forward now to visiting them in their house in Newton.

Zora still marveled at Ellie - how persistent she had been in trying to find her mother's killer. In her mid-thirties and with her own life in danger, Ellie started a search that led to her discovering the killer even as he stalked her and tried to kidnap her. "But she overcame all that -- with a little help from me," Zora said to herself. A chapter closed but never forgotten.* She turned back to the task at hand – getting rid of old papers and organizing her files.

The newspaper clipping, and the card and snapshot slipped out of a dark blue folder, unnoticed. For a few seconds, they lay on the top of her desk, next to all the other papers. Then she saw them. She closed her eyes briefly. Of course she knew what they were. She could almost hear Jane's voice: "You don't have to save all this. It's not important."

She opened her eyes. She knew every word of the article – and of Jane's last Christmas note, written five months before she disappeared. Zora reread the note. "Enjoying retirement and planning to travel next year if I am able – England, first, then maybe Spain. I would love to have Phyllis go with me, but I'm not sure she is quite up to it. What about you? Have a happy Christmas with your family. I promise to come and visit soon." She had enclosed a glossy photo of herself, sitting at a picnic table somewhere near a lake. It was a good likeness. Her smile and cropped blond hair, now turning grey, were very much as Zora remembered her.

The article about Jane's disappearance appeared in the *Columbus Dispatch*, in late May, twelve years ago, and it produced in Zora the same feelings it always did – sadness, followed by guilt. They never found Jane, dead or alive. And what had she, Zora, done to help? Had she pursued the case, as Ellie had done with her mother's death? No. Jane may not have been a relative, but she was a dear friend.

"Well, maybe it's not too late – maybe I should do something *now*." Zora didn't realize she had spoken out loud until she heard the deep voice say, "Maybe you should!" For a dizzying second she thought it was Rashad. She turned from her desk and stared up into the brown eyes of her only son, Roy, *Detective* Roy Erickson.

"Oh, you!" Zora scolded as she rose to give him a hug – all six feet three of him. "You do sound like your father!"

Roy hugged his mother in return, noticing that his arms seemed to go farther around her than the last time he had seen her only four weeks ago. "I don't know what you were thinking about, but I think you should do it, whatever it is. And I don't think you are eating enough – that's why I've come by to take you out to lunch."

Zora straightened her back and looked at him fiercely. "Of course I'm eating enough! I'm a good cook, as you know, and I enjoy my own cooking. I've just been watching what I eat, that's all. Old people have to watch their fat and cholesterol."

"Well, let's forget about that for one day," Roy laughed. "Let's go for some Italian at Benny's." She knew he would say this – it was his favorite restaurant in the Little Italy section of Boston.

"I'm ready!" she said, and picked up the sweater lying on the sofa by her desk. They left her town house and got into Roy's car (not an official police vehicle this time, Zora noted.)

After the short ride, they entered the noisy, fragrant, old-fashioned restaurant in what had once been the meat packing district. It was full of regulars, most of whom were probably there on their Friday lunch breaks, she guessed. After they ordered, Roy looked at his mother – her brown skin smooth almost without wrinkles, her gray hair cut short, her rings, bracelet and earrings perfectly coordinated with her suit. The jewelry pieces were things Rashad had given her, picked out from the international selection at their store and art gallery. He knew she missed all that.

When his father died five years ago, his mother sold the business, saying she was too old at seventy to run it by herself. He wished sometimes that he and his sister had persuaded her to take a partner. He worried that Zora did not have enough to keep herself busy and challenged.

Once they were served, he leaned over the table toward her. "What was it you were saying that maybe you should do when you were talking to yourself back at the house?"

Zora put down her fork and pushed back her plate of risotto. "I don't know if you remember my telling you about my old friend, Jane Hubbard. She disappeared many years ago. I taught with her at the high school back in Dublin, Ohio, before I resigned to marry your father and come here to Boston. That was forty years ago. Jane taught English. We missed each other and always kept up. For years, she lived with her widowed mother and took care of her. Jane never married. I wondered about that. She was a white lady – beautiful, blond, slender. Apart from her mother who died, if I remember correctly, when Jane was in her late fifties, she had no close relatives, except a great aunt and a second cousin, a man. I don't remember ever meeting him. She was also good friends with another English teacher, Phyllis McDonald. Phyllis was two or three years older than we were and a widow. Jane was my age – so she'd be 75 now."

"Honestly, Mom, I don't remember you mentioning her. Sorry if I forgot!" Roy reached over and squeezed his mother's hand.

"Jane retired when she was 62. The school district started a policy that allowed you to retire early if you had at least twenty-five years of service and were 62 or older. I never thought Jane would do that because she loved teaching, but I think the students changed so much that it was no longer such a joy for her. And her mother died a year or so before the retirement, so maybe she wanted to enjoy some freedom. Of course, at the time I thought she couldn't retire because of what happened with her money."

Roy raised his eyebrows, "her money?"

"She was swindled. There was a broker – I never met him. His name was Murray Parch. Don't know if he's still alive. He was younger than Jane, I think, maybe by eight or ten years. He ran his own investment firm. Jane met him through someone in her church and really liked him. At first, he got her into investments that made her a lot of money. Then he left Ohio and for awhile she would only hear from him remotely, but he still managed her money. He told her he was setting up a firm in Denver that would eventually be run by another broker, a friend of his; then, he would move back to Columbus. But it turned out he was a swindler. He gained the confidence of some woman in Denver and swindled her. She took him to court and somehow, he got off, or she dropped the charges, I forget which. He did move back to Columbus. Acted as if nothing had happened. Jane still trusted him. I always wondered if maybe more was going on between them than just investing. I saw a picture of him later in the newspaper – very handsome. I do remember he was married at the time."

Roy signaled the waiter, who poured more coffee for both of them. "What happened to Parch?"

"Jane had a banker friend who helped her figure out why she was losing money on her investments. This was while she was still teaching. She wrote me one very candid letter about what Parch did. He sent her statements that showed he bought investment funds for her, and for awhile he paid her dividends. But then it turned out he had simply been taking most of her money and not investing it. How he did all this and she didn't catch on at first I don't know. Jane was smart. Or maybe she didn't want to know. She finally filed charges against Parch, and for some reason the case dragged on. I guess he had a good lawyer. The next I heard, she was going to retire. On her sixty-second birthday, she did. I didn't feel it was right to ask her if she had enough money to do that – she must have.

Zora looked speculatively at a piece of garlic bread and finally picked it up, taking one small bite.

"She could have stayed on at the school, so she must have felt comfortable enough to retire. I asked Phyllis at the time what she knew about Jane's finances, but Phyllis didn't know anything more than I did. They lived in the same apartment building and were friends, but Jane apparently didn't confide in anyone – at least not Phyllis or me – about what was happening in her personal life."

"Did they ever convict Parch?"

"Yes, but wait. That's part of the story."

Roy took a bite of his veal scaloppini. "Go on – tell me."

"Jane had this older relative – a great aunt – who lived in a nursing home in Chillicothe. That's about forty-five miles south of Columbus. Jane visited this aunt regularly. On a Saturday in late

April the year after she retired, she was going to visit her aunt. She did make the visit, but then no one saw or heard from here again. Phyllis reported her missing after two days, thinking at first that Jane had decided to stay for a few days with a friend in Athens. The friend knew nothing, and the nursing home reported that Jane arrived and left after a short visit that Saturday."

The waitress handed them menus. "Dessert?" They both shook their heads, but Roy pointed to his coffee cup for a refill.

"Did the police suspect Parch right away?"

"Apparently not. They conducted a search for Jane, of course. After several days, they found her car at the back of a drug store parking lot in southeast Columbus, near the airport. There weren't many clues in the car, at least nothing of Jane's, but there were cigarette ashes in the ash tray and one tissue with lipstick on the floor. Jane never smoked, and according to Phyllis, the bright red lipstick smudge couldn't have come from Jane, either, as it wasn't a color she ever wore. They couldn't get any DNA matches, so the trail more or less stopped there."

"You say, 'more or less'. Was there something else they found out later?"

"They dragged the Scioto and the Olentangy rivers but didn't turn up anything. For awhile, the theory was that she had just gone on a trip without telling anyone. Her checking account had some money in it but not much. They couldn't find any unusual activity at her bank, although all her credit cards were missing. No one had used them since the day she left Dublin for Chillicothe. The police interviewed people who knew her. By then, they strongly suspected foul play."

Zora took a sip of water.

"Parch didn't have a good alibi for that morning. His wife testified that he was gone from their house most of the day. He claimed he had been shopping for lawn furniture, but there were no records of any purchases by him. He was already under indictment for swindling Jane, but he wasn't in jail and his trial was scheduled for later that summer. At the trial, the judge found him guilty of the swindling, even without Jane's testimony. When the judge sentenced him, he actually told Parch, 'You not only defrauded Miss Hubbard but there is a reasonable suspicion you may have caused her disappearance. Therefore, I am giving you the maximum sentence I can for the fraud but you probably deserve more.' Parch's lawyer filed a complaint on the basis the judge was biased, but another judge dismissed the appeal. Parch went to prison on a seventeen-year sentence but was out after ten years on parole. He moved to central Florida. His wife divorced him a year after the trial. I don't know where either of them are living now – or even if they are both still alive."

"You do seem to know a lot, though, Mother!"

"What I've just told you was in the all the papers. It all died down after a year or so. I keep in touch with Phyllis. She told me that eventually, the court declared Jane dead and her second cousin handled what was left of Jane's things. He was nice enough to ask Phyllis if she wanted anything from Jane's apartment. She took a picture and a vase that she admired. Phyllis has very occasional contact with him."

"And now, you are thinking of reopening the investigation?" If there was a hint of amusement in Roy's voice, Zora chose to ignore it.

"Yes, I'm *thinking* about it."

"Well, if you do it, I can help you. Put you in touch with the Columbus police department, get you access to records, that kind of thing. It doesn't sound very promising, after all this time. But knowing you, you may find a new angle."

Zora looked at her son. "He doesn't want to tell me he thinks this will be a wild goose chase!" she thought to herself and smiled at him.

He caught her look. "What?"

"I know you don't think I will find out anything, but I appreciate your offer. I just feel like this is something I have to do now. And if I don't, no one else will."

Roy paid the bill and drove Zora back to Cambridge. On the way, he explained what he would do to help her get the investigation started. When he walked her to her door, he asked, "What are you plans for the weekend? I'm on duty both Saturday and Sunday but I know Kressida and the kids would love to see you. I may be able to be free for dinner on Sunday.

"Thanks, dear, but I have a date on Sunday. Ellie and Tyler have invited me to dinner."

"Glad to hear it! We'll have you over the following week. I'll check with Kress about her schedule." Roy leaned down to kiss his mother on her cheek. "I'll get back to you tomorrow with the contact in Columbus."

He bounded down the steps and turned to wave at his mother. "So much like his father," Zora thought for the thousandth time. "Rashad would be proud of him." No time for reminiscences now, however. She had work to do. She hung up her coat, sat down and at her desk, and booted up her laptop. "I can find out a few things for myself, even without the Columbus police," she thought. She brought up Google on her screen.

Read more about Zora and Ellie in the book "Do You See Him Now?" by E. Young

CHAPTER TWO

Ellie brought out the coffee and cups. Tyler poured Cognac into small Baccarat crystal glasses. "We saved this for your birthday!" he announced, handing a glass to Zora.

"But it's not my birthday for three months!" she exclaimed, inhaling the rich aroma.

"I know, but we can pretend, can't we? And we can drink it again when we do celebrate," Ellie added, laughing.

"Well, if that means another invitation, I accept. Dinner was delicious. You'll have to give me the recipe for the trout."

Tyler stretched out his long legs and looked keenly at Zora for a moment. "Do you think you might be in any danger on this mission? That is, of course, assuming that Jane was murdered and that her killer is still alive and free."

"Oh, I'm not worried about that! I really just want to know where they -- he – left Jane. Maybe that sounds ghoulish, but until she's found, it's like everyone has forgotten her and no one cares. I just want to do a little detective work."

"And is this detective work going to take you away from home?" Tyler asked, raising an eyebrow.

"Yes, of course, and I'll probably start in Columbus. After that, I don't know. Roy is helping me get all the facts and files I need to see. I'll make a plan and let you know what it is."

Her friends remained silent for a minute, both remembering how close Ellie had come to injury and possibly death in her own search for her mother's killer the year before. But they knew Zora had made up her mind.

"All right, but let's have some rules about this, shall we?" Ellie asked, with a smile, but her eyes showed concern. "You must check in with Roy or us every day you are away. And if you even sense that somebody is out there trying to stop you, you must come home!"

Zora set down her empty glass, stood up, and reached over to hug Ellie. "You make a great mother hen! Of course, I'll report in. Don't want one detective and two old friends staying up nights worrying about me."

They walked her to the door and Tyler went with her to her car. They hugged before she got in.

"Seriously, Zora, Ellie and I want to know what's going on with this project of yours. We are going to worry, no matter what." He waited while she drove down the driveway and out to the road, waving as she went out of sight.

"I wish she wasn't so set on doing this!" Ellie said as they stood in the kitchen, drying the glasses. Tyler put down the dishtowel and faced Ellie. "We have to remind ourselves not to worry – she's very competent and careful. And we'll keep in touch with Roy if she does start travelling." He turned Ellie around to face him and lowered his head to kiss the soft skin on her neck. "I hope you are right, she said softly, taking him by the hand. "Let's go to bed,"

Later, as they lay in the dark, engulfed in the warmth of each other, Tyler asked the question that had been bothering him since Zora left. "What if Jane Hubbard was killed by someone other than this Parch person? Or even if she finds something to prove Parch did it? After all, he wasn't convicted of murder, even if the judge had his suspicions. If Zora stumbles onto the real killer and he – or she - finds out that Zora knows, isn't there still a chance that she will be in danger?"

Ellie moved closer to him and took his hand in hers. "We'll just have to pray that doesn't happen. I think she'll be very careful. And, actually, Ty, I don't think she'll find out anything, but she wants to try. And that's important to her. I know that."

Tyler remained silent. He trusted his wife's instincts, but he put this one in his "worry basket". He knew it would bother him until Zora found what she was looking for – or could be persuaded to abandon her search.

CHAPTER THREE

Two weeks later, Zora finalized what she wanted to do in Columbus, after which she checked in with her son. "Roy, I've been able to get Jane's file from your friends on the Columbus police force, but that detective who handled the case, Peter Le Gall, hasn't answered my emails. I know he's fully retired," she told her son over the phone one night after she had finished reading all the case records about Jane's disappearance and Parch's arrest. "But, among other things, I need to sit down with Phyllis McDonald for a real conversation. Then, I want to try to retrace Jane's steps – at least what we know of them."

Roy made only a faint objection – he knew better than to try to dissuade his mother from something she was determined to do. "Mom, I worked with Pete Le Gall on a case when I was first on the force here. Even visited Columbus. He'll remember me, I think, and I'm sure he will be willing to talk with you. But while you're there, please text me or call me every day."

"Goodness! Next thing I know, you'll be insisting I carry a gun!" Zora replied, feeling a little put out that everybody was so worried about her. "For an old woman, I'm pretty handy with a baseball bat, you know." She paused. This wasn't kind. Roy just wanted her to be safe. "And I will check in with you every day. I promise," she added in a softer tone.

"When will you leave?"

"As soon as I can get a plane reservation to Columbus. I'll let you know. I'll try to stay at the Marriott in Dublin. It's near Phyllis's apartment. I'll probably be gone only a few days."

Her travel arrangements fell into place quickly, and on the following Friday, at 3 p.m., she pulled out of Port Columbus International Airport in a rented white Toyota Corolla, about to head northwest to Dublin. "Plenty of time to check in, get my bearings, and get to Phyllis's, she observed. But first, she wanted to make a quick detour.

The big chain drug store, looking like it needed a good coat of paint, appeared on the left hand side of the road. Zora turned into the parking lot. She located the dumpster in the far left corner just where the police file pictures showed it. She parked her car and got out. Only three other cars in the lot this time of day. If anyone asked what she was doing, she would say she was trying to get a signal on her phone. But there was no one around to ask anything. She walked around the dumpster and looked back at her rental car, trying to imagine how Jane's blue Chrysler would have looked parked there that day. Hard to believe no one called the police for six days to report an abandoned car, but maybe thirteen years ago people regularly left cars in that lot on a temporary basis?

The police had searched the dumpster. It had, however, been emptied the morning Jane's car was discovered. So, they had gone to the municipal waste removal site and searched there also. No bodies in either place. Somehow, that made Zora feel better. Whatever she found out about Jane, she didn't want to think of her as having been tossed into a dump. She spent another minute looking around the lot, then went into the store. She was curious – could you see the parking area by the dumpster from the store?

"Do you have the *Columbus Dispatch*?" she asked the young woman at the cashier's counter.

"All out today, I'm afraid!" the young woman replied, speaking loudly. "Does she think I'm deaf?" Zora wondered with irritation and then remembered that sometimes being "old" was an advantage.

"Thank you, anyway," she answered, now walking very slowly, as if lame, toward the front doors, giving herself plenty of time to see what part of the parking lot would be visible from inside the store. Not all of it, she realized. Of course the police had interviewed all of the drug store employees who had been working on the day that Jane disappeared and that the car was, presumably, abandoned in the parking lot. They had even found fifteen customers who had made credit card purchases that day, but no one claimed to have seen a blue Chrysler driving into the lot or parked there. The store manager was the one who, six days later, apparently noticed that the car had been in the lot for more than two or three days and called the police.

Zora took a picture of the store and of the parking lot with her phone. Back in the car, she resumed her route toward Dublin. Traffic on Highway 270 going northwest moved swiftly ahead of rush hour. She arrived at the Marriott shortly after 4 p.m. An hour later, she was knocking on Phyllis McDonald's door at Oak Manor, having been buzzed in from the desk downstairs. She noted with approval that the building looked well maintained, with geraniums alongside the walk in front and fresh beige paint on the hallway walls.

"Zora! Come in, come in!" Zora had not seen Phyllis for almost twenty years, and she was shocked at the older woman's appearance. Phyllis' dark eyes sparkled, and her voice was strong, but her once tall, upright body seemed to have shrunk. She leaned heavily on the cane in her right hand, and her skin looked paper thin. Zora hoped her dismay did not show in her face.

"Phyllis! So good to see you. Thank you for this invitation on such short notice."

"Nonsense! It is I who should be thanking you. I don't see that many visitors these days, and it will be wonderful to catch up. Do you still like wine? I have a few nice bottles. Come in to the living room."

Zora followed her into a spacious room decorated with plants, books and a few small, framed drawings that looked like originals. Then she remembered that Phyllis' late husband had been a weekend artist. She made a mental note to comment on them later.

"Sit in that comfortable chair! Or would you like to see my wine selection? I have a wine chest in the kitchen."

"I'll follow you." Zora did not want to even think about Phyllis balancing a glass of wine and navigating with it between rooms. "I wonder how well she gets along, she seems so crippled," Zora thought.

As they entered the large, white-walled kitchen, Phyllis added, "I don't do much cooking anymore – just an egg for breakfast, but Annie comes five days a week to clean and fix me lunch and dinner. And frozen dinners are wonderful. So I get along quite well. My niece, who now lives in Cincinnati, gets here as often as she can, and we go out. I enjoy that."

"Would you like to go out tonight? I have a comfortable rental car, and you can pick somewhere you like."

Phyllis smiled and squeezed Zora's arm. "No – tonight you get a home-cooked, gourmet meal, courtesy of Annie. She actually has a culinary degree. There's a very good cassoulet ready to be heated up, a lovely vegetable salad, French bread, brie, and a lemon tart for dessert. I thought it would be easier to talk if we stayed here, so Annie cooked. She's truly a gift."

Two wine glasses appeared. "You choose something!" Phyllis pointed to the wine chest. Zora bent over to open it and selected an Italian Pinot Grigio. "Good – one of my favorites," Phyllis exclaimed and opened the bottle for them.

Zora carried the glasses back to the living room, placed them on the glass coffee table next to a cloisonné bowl of nuts, and sat down in the overstuffed chair in front of the window, noting that the blue velvet chair across from it had a lap robe over the back - obviously Phyllis' chair.

"Now, let's catch up. You first," Phyllis offered. Zora made her story as brief as possible. They had, after all, kept up with occasional letters, emails, and the phone calls. Phyllis surprised Zora by announcing she had written a book of poetry and it was about to be published by a major New York house. On hearing that news, Zora got up to give her older friend a hug. "I hope you will send me one of the first copies," she said sincerely.

Their conversation continued back into the small dining area, where Annie had thoughtfully set up two places for dinner. Zora offered to do the heating, dishing up and serving of all the food, which Phyllis gratefully accepted. Over dinner, Phyllis inquired about Zora's family. When Zora reviewed the details about selling the business, Phyllis leaned over and patted Zora's hand. "I know how much you must miss Rashad. I always thought you and he led such a stimulating life – the collecting, the travelling all over Latin America and Canada and even Africa! And, of course, your wonderful gallery and store."

"I do miss him, of course, and the life we had, but I try now to live in the present and plan for the future. Boston is a good place to be, for me. Friends, music, art, plenty of things to do and see. She paused. It was always hard to think of the rest of her years being alone, but she quickly put that thought out of her mind. It was only when they were both enjoying another glass of wine that Phyllis said, "What can I tell you about Jane after all this time that will help?"

Zora paused. So many things she wanted to know but what, really, could Phyllis tell her?

"Right before she disappeared, did you sense anything different about Jane? I mean, you knew her so well."

Phyllis took a small sip of wine. "No, not really." She stopped, fingered her wine glass, stared at it. "I mean, no, I didn't notice anything different, but no, too, I don't think now that maybe I ever knew her that well."

She saw the surprise in Zora's eyes. Instead of explaining, she posed her own question. "How well did you know her?"

Zora sat back in her chair. "Less well than you, I would have thought. You know, we were all teaching at that school at the same time for only three years. I knew she had never married, that she was brilliant in graduate school, that her students here loved her, that she favored nineteenth century novelists. But I also remember she was the most knowledgeable person about Faulkner that I ever knew, and she loved plays – especially those by Tennessee Williams."

Phyllis smiled. "Yes, that's all true. And I did think Jane and I were close. But Jane was reserved. There was one time – and sometimes now I think I am imagining it – that she told me something deeply personal. And one other thing that came up later about her that maybe I never understood."

Zora handed the bread basket over the table and waited.

"Did you know she had an affair with one of her graduate school professors, when she was in Illinois?"

Zora shook her head.

" We went out to dinner and a movie one night, then back to my house for coffee. Dwight was still alive then, but he was out of town. I don't remember the name of the movie – except that it was a romance and involved a single woman and a married man. Anyway, Jane began to talk about the plot, to find things wrong with it. And I must have said something like 'how would you know?' and she answered fiercely. 'I do know, I do.' And then she told me that while she was getting her master's degree in Illinois, she fell in love with one of her professors. What I do remember is that she said, 'he wasn't much older than I was.' I was too surprised to press her, except I must have said something like, 'what happened?' 'I knew it was wrong. He went back to his wife.' That's all I remember. I never asked about a name, and she never told me. She never talked about him again. But I did wonder why she never married. You remember Alex Bonner who taught geography with us?"

Zora nodded.

"They went out once in awhile. But Alex was gay. He was in the closet then, but I guess we all knew – or suspected. He and Jane both liked theatre and music, and I suppose they had a good time together. Alex retired to California – I think he finally found a partner there. And I never knew Jane to date another man in all the years we taught or after we retired."

"You said there was one other thing that happened later that perhaps you didn't understand?"

"Yes. There was. You had left Ohio. I'm not sure how much you knew about what was going on at the school after that. We had a young Spanish teacher join the faculty about two years after you left."

"Actually, I do recall that – you, or maybe Jane, wrote me something. What was her name?"

"Julia Lefkowitz. She was in her twenties, from some small town in Kansas or Iowa. I think this was her first teaching position. Very beautiful and bright, but she always seemed a little naïve and vulnerable to me. Jane befriended her. I don't remember much about Julia's background. I think she had lost both parents, had inherited a little money. At least she had money from somewhere. She looked up to Jane, although she was friendly with all of us. What I do remember is that one time in the lunch room in the faculty lounge, shortly after she came, she asked us about investing. It seemed a rather personal question, but, again, she didn't have any close family or friends in Columbus. Jane went on and on about the importance of handling money conservatively and offered to introduce Julia to her – Jane's – broker. After that, I remember they saw a great deal of each other. Jane always seemed protective of Julia. Not that I'm implying anything other than a friendship. But then the dreadful thing happened."

Zora sat quietly. She felt she should clear the plates, but not at this moment.

"Julia taught at our school for almost three years. I heard enough to know that she followed Jane's advice and invested her money with Murray Parch. And then, not from Julia but from another teacher, I heard that all of Julia's money was lost. This was about the time when Parch came back from Colorado, and, as we know now, he got in trouble with a client there. Jane never talked about her own money or what Parch did to her, but three weeks before school was to let out that spring, Julia hung herself in a closet of her house. We were all devastated. There was no suicide note. When it came to light that Parch had swindled her, we all thought we knew the reason she died. But Jane, who was closer to her than anyone else it seemed, only spoke of it once – at least to me. It was another night when we were alone together, this time at her apartment. We had dinner and some wine. We were talking about something else, and out of the blue, Jane said, 'He killed her, you know.' I was too shocked to even ask what she meant. But she went on, almost as if I wasn't there. 'He took her money, like he took mine, and maybe he took more than that from her, and she couldn't bear it. She couldn't.' "

"How did Jane sound when she told you this? Was she emotional?"

"No, that was the strange thing. I remember that her voice was flat when she said 'he killed her'. For a minute, I thought she meant it literally. In fact, to be honest, to this day, I'm not sure that she didn't mean it that way. That maybe she thought Murray Parch had put a noose around Julia's neck. Do you think that's possible?"

Zora stood up. She needed to walk around. "I'll clear the table. Where will I find that lemon tart?"

"I'll help." Phyllis got up slowly, reaching for her cane. The two women moved toward the kitchen, not speaking. Zora found the tart in the refrigerator, located clean plates, cut and served pieces. She carried them back to the table. They both sat down.

"Phyllis, if Jane really thought he killed Julia, why didn't she go to the police?"

"I've asked myself that question a hundred times since that night. I've come to the conclusion that she didn't mean it literally. That she meant he had done something so bad that Julia took her own life. That she may have meant he had swindled her but also had an affair with Julia and then abandoned her. I just don't know."

"But was there ever a police investigation of her death?"

"Yes, but superficial, if you ask me. I was interviewed. So were some of the others, and certainly Jane. But I never heard that anything came of it. The newspaper obituary was short. It just referred to Julia having died. No explanation. No one came to the school to claim her things. School was almost out when it happened. They brought in a substitute teacher. By the next fall, they had hired a young man to teach the Spanish classes. It was almost like Julia never existed."

They finished their dessert in silence. "I'll make coffee if you would like some," Phyllis offered as she pushed back her plate. "I have a Kuerig so it's easy. You can choose a flavor."

When Zora carried the coffees back to the living room – French vanilla for her, a dark roast for Phyllis – she knew that she should not overstay her welcome on this first evening but she had several questions that she wanted to ask Phyllis.

"Phyllis, do you remember anyone, ever, who might have had a reason to harm Jane?"

Phyllis stared into her coffee cup for a few seconds and then raised her eyes. "No. Except for Murray Parch. And I've thought about that all this time, too." She paused and then continued. "I suppose that if Parch's wife thought Jane was having an affair with him, she could have wanted Jane out of the way. And I have thought – and this pretty far-fetched – that the wife of that graduate school professor who had the affair with Jane might have been angry. But so many years later?" She shook her head.

"What about a former student? Anyone who could have carried a grudge? Anyone who might have thought Jane harmed him – or her – but Jane wouldn't have been suspicious?"

"I don't see it. Jane was not a naïve person. But I never heard from her or anybody else that a student – or former student – might have been a threat to her. You know, she tutored some of them on the side, just to help them and never accepted money. Even some of the rowdier boys seemed to like her and appreciate her. And there was one boy – I forget his name – he'd gotten into some kind of trouble. I think his mother was a drug addict or something, and he had little support at home. Jane got him a lawyer, went with him to court. He was finally exonerated. Jane could be like that – once she believed something was the right thing to do, she stuck with it. But no one at school had any problems with her that I know of, so it's hard for me to see how her death had anything to do with her teaching."

"The strange thing, it seems to me, was about her car. You know they found it in the parking lot of a drug store. I drove in there today on my way from the airport. There's an area of the parking lot that you can't see very well from the store. Maybe someone got in her car there, attacked her? Do you know if it was a place she would have shopped?"

"Out near the airport? No, I cannot imagine that. We had two good drug stores right here in Dublin even then, and I know she got prescriptions filled at one of them. Of course, she might have needed something while in the eastern part of Columbus, but it seems unlikely. And they found that lipstick on a tissue in her car. They showed it to me. I told them it wasn't her lipstick. I could never figure that out either."

Zora could see Phyllis' eye lids began to droop. She stood up. "It's getting late, and we've had a long evening. Dinner was wonderful – I hope to meet your Annie and compliment her! I plan to drive to Chillicothe tomorrow and do some more investigating. Why don't I pick you up for dinner tomorrow evening, and I can tell you what I've found out? My plan is to fly home Sunday unless I find something that looks like a good lead and I need more time here."

Phyllis struggled to her feet, holding her cane tightly. "I wish we could talk all night. I'd like to hear more about your family. But it was wonderful seeing you, Zora. Yes, I'd love to go to dinner with you tomorrow. Just call me with the details. I'll be here!" She embraced Zora warmly and hobbled to the door with her. "Drive safely tomorrow! Traffic's worse around here than it used to be. And stay off 270 – Jane hated that road, you remember?"

CHAPTER FOUR

Her map software showed that the drive from Oak Manor to the nursing home in Chillicothe should take sixty minutes. "I'll start from the Manor at 9:00 a.m." Jane usually left at that time on Saturdays, according to Phyllis, and Zora wanted to retrace Jane's steps as closely as possible. "Of course, there'll be more traffic now than there was then. And she wouldn't have taken 270 - she didn't like the beltway."

Before leaving the hotel, Zora checked her work bag: tablet, paper map, camera, pencil and paper, extra glasses, cell phone, the new business cards she had ordered just for this project, two bottles of water and an energy bar.

When she arrived at Oak Manor, she pulled over and brought up the map page on her phone. She had programmed in all her planned stops - they were places the police had checked thirteen years ago. As Zora explained to Roy before she left Boston, "Of course, I don't know why she would have stopped at all. Jane was a good driver. She made the trip to Chillicothe to visit her old aunt regularly, so she knew the way. And Jane was organized - she would have put gas in the car and had everything she needed before she started out. Still, somehow, someone got her out of her car and got control of it. Or, otherwise, why would the police have found it in the parking lot of a drug store near the airport? That wasn't even on her route that morning."

Zora drove five miles before getting to her first planned stop, a gas station just off Riverside Drive in Upper Arlington. On this Saturday morning, cars were lined up at the pumps. Zora decided that while it was worth investigating, she could do that on the way back. She knew the chances of finding out anything at all here - or anywhere else - after thirteen years were very slim. But, this was part of what she knew she must do. Dig, dig deeper than the police had.

When she reached Fifth Avenue, she turned east to work her way over to Highway 23. This was a calculated guess, because it meant driving right through downtown Columbus, but it kept her off the interstates. She imagined that Jane would not have been in any particular hurry and might even have stopped to pick up something for her aunt. "Maybe in German Village?" It was on the way, and it had enticing shops, including food stores and restaurants. "Jane loved chocolate – maybe she stopped to buy some for her aunt." Zora decided to stop in the Village on her way back.

Once she drove out of town and crossed the beltway, there weren't any stops she could identify that would be worth visiting until she reached Circleville, "the pumpkin capital of the world", she remembered wryly. Not too many tourists this time of year. Lots of gas stations along the highway, all but one of which were new within the last ten years. The oldest one, an independent, was on her list. Now, it showed peeling paint on the building and cracks in the concrete. "Not a likely place for Jane to stop but then maybe it looked better thirteen years ago." Still, the police had asked questions here. Another place to check later.

Following the electronic map, she turned into the parking lot of the St. Stephen's Home at 10:25 a.m. She parked in the lot marked "visitors", noting only five other cars there. Further along, she saw a sign for "staff parking". For a few minutes, she sat in her car, studying the three-story building and the surroundings. Large pine trees framed the parking lot, and a long, shrub-lined walk led to the front door. Plantings included blooming bushes and seasonal flowers, and the place looked pleasant although modest. Two old men in wheelchairs sat on the lawn near the front of the building. While she sat in her car, no one came or left the building. "Not visiting hours, I guess."

Zora deliberately gave no one advance notice of her visit. Her reasoning was simple: after all this time, what interest would the present management have in the investigation of the disappearance of someone related to a patient now dead for twelve years? She did not want to be turned away even before she got through the door. At the desk, she saw no one, but a framed sign read "Back in five minutes. If an emergency, please ring bell." A small bell was embedded in the counter, next to the sign. Zora waited, looking around. The lobby was small and furnished with old-fashioned stuffed chairs and a sofa in a paisley print. A TV played in one corner – some sort of home and garden show. Despite her worst fears about nursing homes, Zora detected no bad smells or cooking odors, although she knew from the web site that the kitchen and dining room were on the first floor.

She was contemplating ringing the bell when a smiling, plump, nearly bald man in a tight black suit emerged from the office behind the reception desk. He had a nametag, reading "B. Sommers" pinned to his jacket. "Sorry, had to make a phone call," he said, speaking loudly. Zora smiled to herself and resisted saying, "I am not hard of hearing." Instead, she said in a softer tone. "That's quite all right. My name is Zora Erickson."

"Mrs. Erickson! How may I help you? Are you here to see one of our clients?" Zora thought with amusement that he was probably wondering if she had come to apply for a room.

"Not exactly, Mr. Sommers. Do you have a minute?" She glanced around the lobby. A dark-skinned woman in a blue uniform was cleaning windows, but no one else was around.

"Yes, please come into my office. I'll leave the door open, if you don't mind. I can see the desk if anyone comes." He opened the door behind the reception desk and ushered her in. There were two chairs. They both sat down. Mr. Sommers leaned forward and looked intently at Zora.

"Thank you for talking with me. You see, I had a very close friend, Jane Hubbard, who used to come here to visit her great aunt, Beatrice Levine. I believe Mrs. Levine died eleven years ago. But my friend, Jane, disappeared the year before that. The last place she was seen apparently was here when she visited Mrs. Levine. No one claimed to have heard anything from her after that. A good friend reported her missing two days later. Her car was abandoned in a drug store parking lot in Columbus, near the airport. Jane has never been found, and the case is still open. I am retired now and I have felt for a long time that I should try to find out what happened to Jane."

"I am very sorry about your friend. I have only been here five years myself. The manager before me was here three years before he became ill and had to retire. And the woman who would have been here when Mrs. Levine was here has retired to Arizona. Did the police interview her?"

"They did, and she apparently could not tell them anything more than that Jane made her visit and left as usual. Mrs. Levine was in the early stages of dementia and her conversation with the police was not very helpful."

"And what, exactly, do you hope to find out now, after all this time?" His tone was not unkind but he was clearly puzzled.

"I'm not sure. I have a friend who just found her mother's murderer after searching more than twenty years – and I have decided if she could do that, perhaps I can find out what happened to Jane. My son is a detective. He's been helping me with the investigation." Zora realized that this perhaps sounded a bit pompous – was what she was doing really an investigation? Yes, she decided, it was. Exactly that.

"Well, I'm happy . . ." he was interrupted by the window cleaner poking her head into the office.

"Ah, Mrs. Elijah, honey, not in here today. I'm talking with somebody right now. Thank you." Mrs. Elijah withdrew, looking curiously at Zora before she trudged out of the office.

"Forgive me. She used to be a fulltime employee. She's a widow and has no family. We keep her on here – room and board, and she does some work. She's a bit slow mentally but loves to do windows. And the clients like her." He shifted in his chair and peered through the door to be sure no one was waiting for him. "As I was going to say, I will help you in any way I can, but I'm not sure what that would be. Would you like me to put you in touch with our former manager, the one in Arizona? I'm sure she would be willing to talk with you."

"Thank you. I appreciate that. I have her name and do plan to call her. At this point, I'm just trying to see where Jane would have gone, to figure out what she might have done on that last day. There were clues – lipstick smudges on tissues in her car. Ashes in the ashtray. But no one the police talked to told them anything helpful. At least nothing that helped to find Jane."

"Is it possible she's still alive?" He seemed really interested now; he leaned closer to Zora to hear her answer.

"It doesn't seem likely," she said, not wanting to acknowledge that she believed it very unlikely. From the beginning of this, she felt that saying out loud that Jane was dead would make it a reality. "But I need to go back over the things the police did – and maybe some they didn't." She paused. "Perhaps you could show me Mrs. Levine's room?"

"Of course." He stood and moved out toward the desk. "Let me look up the records so I can see which one it is. We are fully occupied at the moment so there will be a client in it, but I'm sure we can give you a peek."

He tapped his computer and in less than a minute picked up the house phone. "Mrs. Chavez, I have someone here who would like to look at Room 315 – she has a relative who might want to join us at some point. What? All right, I'll send her up. Her name is Mrs. Erickson."

"You can take the elevator – it's over there. The third floor. Mrs. Chavez is on the desk there and she will show you Mrs. Levine's former room – 315. And I'll be happy to talk with you when you come back if there's anything further."

A couple was coming in the front door now, and Mr. Sommers turned his attention to them. "May I help you?"

Zora found the elevator and was on the third floor moments later. Her first impression was of brightness. Pink walls, doors wide open, sunlight coming in through the windows. She introduced herself to Mrs. Chavez, who briskly walked her down the hall to room 315. "Our client is out of the room right now, so please come in," she offered.

"Thank you, I'll just take a quick look." Not knowing what she expected to find, Zora nevertheless entered and looked around. A pleasant room with gaily colored chairs and pillows on the bed. Nothing remarkable. "This is very nice," she said, remembering that she was supposed to be looking at it as a prospective place for her "relative". Then, "How long have you been working here?" she asked, turning to Mrs. Chavez.

"Eight years. I like it. Before that, I worked in Toledo." They walked back toward the elevator. "I think your relative would like it here." She clearly felt the visit was over. Zora could not think of anything else to ask or say. She thanked Mrs. Chavez and returned to the lobby. Mr. Sommers was talking animatedly with the couple who had come in as Zora was going upstairs. She did not want to interrupt, so as she passed the desk, she merely said, "thank you," and continued toward the door.

"Mrs. Erickson – just a minute!" Mr. Sommers popped out from behind the reception desk. "If there anything else we can do for you? Do you want to leave me your name and a contact number?"

Zora felt no need to do that but didn't feel it would do any harm. She took a business card out of her purse and handed it to him. "Thank you for talking with me. Please let me know if you think of anything else. I appreciate it."

As she walked to her car, she noticed that the two men in the wheelchairs had been joined by an ambulatory, rather heavy-set woman wearing a pink uniform. There were all talking together and Zora heard laughter. "A happy place, I guess," she thought, still quite sure she would not want to be living here – or anywhere like it.

As Zora reached in her purse for the car keys just before she got to her rental car, she saw a flash of blue cloth. She stopped. The slightly bent over figure of Mrs. Elijah emerged from behind a pine tree. Instinctively, Zora looked around. No one else in sight. The window cleaner stopped, too. The two women looked at each other. "Mrs. Elijah, what are you doing here?" It was all Zora could think of to say.

"She was nice. A very kind lady. She gave me chocolates." The window cleaner was nodding her head vigorously. She looked at Zora and slowly smiled. "I heard you ask about her. She was nice."

Again Zora looked around. No one was within earshot or even watching them. "Mrs. Elijah, please come and sit with me in my car. I'm Zora Erickson. I would like to talk with you. Please." Zora opened the passenger side door and made a gesture. The other woman hesitated and then moved quickly to get in. Zora left the door open and got into the driver's seat. "Now, please tell me who you are talking about. Was it Mrs. Levine?"

The woman shook her head in a vigorous "no". "It was Miss Jane. Miss Jane. She cared about people. She was nice to me." That seemed to satisfy her need to share, and she leaned back in the car seat.

"Did Miss Jane come here often? Did you see her when she came?" Zora felt a tingle in her neck and arms. Was this going to lead to anything? How much could this woman know or remember?

"I saw her. I always saw her. She gave me chocolates. Out here – in the parking lot. I liked her." More nodding, this time affirmatively. Zora repressed a desire to follow up with more questions. She waited. Then: "But that last time she didn't give me any." Now the tingling sensation reached Zora's stomach.

"What do you mean 'that last time'? Did you see her and she didn't give you chocolates?"

The nodding stopped. Mrs. Elijah dropped her head. "In her car. I saw her in her car. There was a lady in it, maybe a lady. Never saw her before. They drove away. I read about her. They couldn't find her. They think she died. Maybe somebody killed her. I was sad."

Zora bit her tongue. So important to get this right, and she didn't want to scare this woman. "Mrs. Elijah, what you are telling me is very important. It could help us find Miss Jane. Are you saying you saw her in her car, here, but someone was in the car with her and then Miss Jane did not see you or talk to you or give you chocolates? Did she drive away?"

Mrs. Elijah's head bobbed up again. Nodding as if to say "yes". "I saw her. I saw her get into the car with the other lady. The other lady was driving. The car went away."

"Did you ever seen Miss Jane again here?"

Nodding, "no".

"Are you sure?"

Nodding, "yes".

"Did you ever tell anybody else about this? Did you talk to the police?"

Silence. Then, clearly, "No. They never talked to me. I didn't like to talk to police." Long pause. "I was scared. I wasn't supposed to be spying."

"But you weren't spying. You were looking for your friend, Miss Jane, and you saw something very, very important. Do you think you can remember what the person looked like who was in the car with Miss Jane? Was it someone from the home here?"

A frown. Silence. Fidgeting hands. "Not from here. Nobody I saw before."

"How can you be sure? Where were you when you saw the car?"

A sly smile came over the woman's face. "Here. By the cars. Behind that tree. Waiting for Miss Jane. It was Saturday. She came on Saturdays. With chocolates."

So Mrs. Elijah had been close -- perhaps just a few feet away, if any of this was true.

"Do you know how the other lady got here? How did she get to Miss Jane's car? Did she walk from the home?"

"Don't know. Maybe a taxi. I see taxis come here sometimes."

"Do you remember what the person looked like who got into the car with Miss Jane?"

A frown of concentration. "It was a long time ago." Zora waited. "She was a white lady. She had big hands. A hat. Glasses- black glasses."

"Do you mean dark glasses, like sun glasses?"

More nodding, "yes".

"Do you remember anything else about this lady? Did you hear her talk to Miss Jane, or did Miss Jane talk to her?"

"Couldn't hear. The door slammed. Car went away. I had to go back to work."

"And you're sure you didn't tell anyone until today? Why are you telling me?"

For the first time, the woman turned squarely in the seat and looked directly at Zora. "You're nice, like she was. You are her friend. You're trying to find her. I miss her."

Zora felt a lump forming in her throat. Here was the first real break-through, and from someone who clearly wanted to help. But it was so little information, and how could she be sure any of it was true?

"Mrs. Elijah, you have been a real help. You have told me something that may help us find Miss Jane. Would you mind if I shared what you just told me with the police? My son is a police detective. He is nice, too. Nothing will happen to you. I promise."

A look of fear came over the woman's face. "No! Don't tell! I'll get in trouble."

Zora reached over for her hand and squeezed it. "All right. I will not tell anyone that I talked with you. I will tell the police that someone saw Miss Jane with another person in her car. That may help. You have helped a lot. You haven't done anything wrong. Please don't worry."

Without another word, the woman climbed out of the car and started walking back into the trees. Clearly, she had been to this parking lot before – if any of her story could be believed. Zora sat for a few minutes without starting the engine, thinking about what she just heard. Another woman was wuth Jane – maybe. Big hands, a hat, dark glasses – possibly a man disguised? Mrs. Elijah didn't say anything about violence. Did Jane know the person in the car?

Finally, Zora decided to drive back to Columbus and Dublin, stopping on her way at the places on her list – the places the police had already investigated, plus one other stop she had in mind – in German Village.

CHAPTER FIVE

No one at the Circleville gas station knew anything about a customer who might have stopped there thirteen years ago and they had no records. Zora left the gas station and drove back north, where she parked directly across from the shop, "German Chocolate and Bakery". Since her days in Ohio, this favorite Columbus shop had doubled in size. Several metal tables and chairs were perched on the sidewalk, all filled with people drinking coffee or tea and eating pastries. Zora realized she was hungry. "Maybe I'll get something later." The tables were all occupied. The clerks looked busy, so she browsed the shelves of coffees and candy until a young, smiling clerk in a white uniform came up to her.

"If you are looking for coffee, I can recommend several if you tell me what blend you like."

Zora smiled broadly. "That's kind of you. I may buy some later. But right now, I'm looking for some information." The clerk continued smiling but cocked her head. "Yes?"

"I think a friend of mine, a very close friend, used to come here. We both lived in Dublin at the time. A little more than twelve years ago, she disappeared. The police have never discovered what happened to her. I am doing my own investigating. It's possible that she bought something here the day she went missing. So, I would like to talk with anyone who might have worked here then – if there is anyone."

The clerk took a step back, and stared at Zora for a moment and then said, "Well, I'm not sure who that would be! Let me ask our manager. Please wait here." Without another word, she turned and walked toward the back of the store.

It took a few minutes, but finally a very plump, pleasant looking woman with red hair and a red dress strode down the aisle toward Zora. "Hello! I'm Velma Dowd. I'm the store manager. I understand you want some information about a former customer of ours? May I invite you to join me for a cup of coffee? I have a table in my office."

Zora followed Velma to the back of the store and into a small but neat office that included a desk, filing cabinets, and a table with two chairs. A stainless steel coffee maker sat on top of a low bookshelf, along with a plate of pastries. "Or would you prefer tea?" Velma asked as they sat down.

"Coffee's fine and just black, thanks."

Velma moved the plate of pastries to the table and poured the coffee. A distinct aroma of chocolate wafted up from their cups. "This is our daily special – it's from Kenya. I hope you like it. Please help yourself to our scones – they are wonderful! Now, tell me how I can help you."

Zora told her story as briefly as she could, ending by saying, "I doubt you'd have kept any records from so far back, but it might help if we knew Jane had shopped here that day. I'm just trying to trace her movements."

Velma sat back and took a sip of her coffee. "I was working here then, and we actually do have records of sales that go back for years. We always kept files for repeat customers so we could have a record of products they liked. Lots of those are on the computer now, but I think files from the time you are talking about may still be in our paper archives. How soon do you need the information?"

"If you have anything, I would be grateful to get it anytime that is convenient." Zora took out one of her business cards and handed it to Velma.

"Well, it might take a few days as we store the files in a warehouse off site. But it won't be any trouble – that is, if we have anything." She paused to reach for a scone. "Can you tell me a bit more about your friend? I would have worked here for two years about that time."

Zora reached into her purse and drew out the photograph Jane had enclosed in one of her Christmas letters, showing her at the table near the unnamed lake. "This would have been taken about a year before she disappeared," she said, handing the picture to Velma, who reached for the glasses on her desk and adjusted them. She looked up, startled, "Why, it's Jane Austen!"

Zora felt embarrassed – "No, her name is actually Jane Hubbard."

"Oh, I know, but this is the lady who was reading Jane Austen's books."

Zora raised her eyebrows. Velma continued. "I don't think I ever knew her name. I worked Saturdays back then, and she used to come in sometimes on Saturday mornings and buy something – chocolate candy usually, if I remember. Then, she would sometimes come by later in the day and sit out front and have coffee, and she always had a book. So, I asked her once what she was reading, and she said 'Jane Austen – I'm always finding new things in her writing.' I asked her once what Jane Austen she would recommend, and she said 'Sense and Sensibility'. I got it and read it, too. Enjoyed it."

"She taught English."

"Well, I didn't know that, but I do remember her."

"Did she always come in alone? Do you remember anyone else with her?"

"No, but then she might have come in when I wasn't here. I worked weekday afternoons and all day Saturday in those days."

"Do you think you would remember exactly when you last saw her?"

Velma wrinkled her forehead. "No, I'm sorry. We never had all that much conversation, and it was a long time ago. But I will check with our warehouse and get those old customer files. If I can find out when she made her last purchase here, will that really help you?"

"It might. If you could let me know what the records show, if they exist, I would be very grateful."

Velma did not get right up; instead, she looked intently at Zora. "What do you think happened to her?"

Zora returned the direct gaze. "I don't know, of course. I wish I could persuade myself that she just disappeared – that maybe she's still alive. But that doesn't seem likely. And if she's gone, I want to know who did it. For her sake. No one should just disappear and be forgotten."

"Then I'm sure you will find out," Velma said firmly and reached over to pat Zora's hand. "And if I can help, I will. She was a very nice person."

"Thank you – and for the coffee and scone. I remember how good everything here always was – it still is!"

As she left the shop, Zora thought that she hadn't learned much during this visit, as pleasant as it was. "Well, I have a few more stops to make. Maybe something else will be more productive."

But the other places on her list that the police had originally checked yielded nothing useful. No one remembered the blond lady from so many years ago, and no one had kept records of transactions from that time. She felt frustrated that she had only turned up two very tenuous clues: some person drove away with Jane from St. Stephen's Home, and Jane maybe stopped in the chocolate shop that day. It might help to know if that was before or after her visit to her aunt.

Jane looked at her watch as she neared the Marriott. Just time to take a shower and dress for dinner with Phyllis, who would be eager to hear about Zora's day. She only wished she had more to tell her friend.

CHAPTER SIX

Zora's flight back to Boston on Sunday was scheduled to leave at 3:00 p.m. Zora had made one appointment for Sunday morning – with Detective First Class Peter Le Gall, now retired from the Columbus police force. After repeated attempts, she had finally been able to contact him, and he had agreed to meet with her. The meeting was scheduled for the lobby restaurant of the Dublin Marriott at 10 a.m. When Zora got off the elevator, she saw him – at least she assumed it was him – standing by the entrance to the restaurant. She noticed three things right away: he was tall and stood with a soldier-like posture; his short, wiry hair was graying; and he bore a superficial resemblance to her late husband, Rashad. When she was corresponding with him before the trip, she had formed a mental image of a short, heavy-set white man with thick glasses. "Wrong," she said to herself.

He was obviously staring at her as she approached, but he made no move toward her. Instead, Zora walked briskly up to him, and offered him her hand. "I'm Zora Erickson," she said, looking for a hint of a smile and saw none. He offered a brisk, impersonal handshake. "Pete Le Gall."

"I asked for a table where we could have some privacy," she said, nodding to the hostess, who took her name and seated them near the back wall.

"Orange juice?" the young waitress who immediately came to their table asked.

"Just coffee, black," Le Gall said, not looking at the menu placed before him.

"I'll take orange juice, thank you, and black coffee. And cinnamon toast," Zora answered, thinking that this interview was not going to be easy.

"It's really good of you to take time out to see me, Detective," Zora said, taking another good look at him, not mentioning that she was annoyed about his ignoring her first several emails. What was he – probably early seventies? Roy had told her Le Gall retired from the force seven years ago."

"I go by Pete," he replied, now looking directly at her but with no smile.

"And I'm Zora," she said.

There was a moment of silence while they both savored their first sip of the strong, black coffee. Zora usually didn't drink orange juice – "too much sugar" – but today she was enjoying it.

"I really appreciate your agreeing to meet me this morning. My apologies to your wife and family for taking you away on a Sunday."

"No apologies needed. My daughter is five hundred miles away, in Michigan, and my wife died ten years ago." His face still looked expressionless.

Without even thinking about it, Zora reached over and briefly laid her hand on his. "I'm so sorry. I didn't know. It's hard to lose one's partner." Maybe Roy had told Pete about Rashad? And if he hadn't, Zora didn't feel like saying anything more right now.

He didn't move. "Yes. It is. I think living alone is hard to get used to." He paused. "I remember working with your son, Roy. I hope he is doing well."

She nodded. "He is, thank you. And he remembers you."

Another pause. Then, Pete said , "You wrote that you want to talk about the investigation into Ms. Hubbard. The station tells me they sent you all the files. The case as closed after we did exhaustive investigations. What do you want from me?"

Zora sat back in her chair, marshalling her thoughts about how to summarize anything she knew that he would not have known from the original investigation.

"Well, I went to St. Stephen's in Chillicothe – you know, the home where Jane's great aunt was living. There is a woman there, a Mrs. Elijah, she's really both a resident and worker. She overhead me asking about Jane. As I was leaving, she came out to the parking lot and waited for me. I suspect she's what we used to call a little "slow" but she seemed to remember that she saw Jane in her car with a woman on that last day Jane visited the home. From her description, though, the person could have been a man in disguise. She said the person had "big hands".

"We didn't interview any 'Mrs. Elijah'. Was she sure she saw another woman in the car? Did she overhear any of their conversation or hear a name?"

Zora shook her head. "She did say she had not talked to the police. So all of this might be some fantasy she had. Apparently, Jane used to bring her chocolates, so she liked her. I take it you didn't interview anyone else at the home who saw Jane with a mysterious person?"

"No, and I wish we had known about Mrs. Elijah, but her memory might not be totally reliable." He paused just as the waitress brought Zorz's toast. "Have you uncovered anything else?"

"Only that Jane used to stop by the German Chocolate and Bakery Shop, and there is still one person there who vaguely remembers her. She is now the manager. She's going to check their archived records to see if they have any sales slips or receipts with Jane's name that could tell us when she was last there – it may even be that she stopped there on the day she disappeared."

Pete stared at her and then leaned in closer. "So, no one at the home knows anything, and your Mrs. Elijah may not remember anything that was real. She may have stopped at a store in Columbus. Is that all you've found out?" Zora felt his tone was just short of belligerent. "And maybe I can't blame him – here I am, an old woman, coming to horn in on a case that was his. He must resent me." She was beginning to regret having asked him for a meeting.

They both sat in silence for a few minutes. She wondered if he was going to end the conversation and simply leave. Then he refilled his own coffee cup and Zora's and frowned. "There are two things that always bothered me about this case. We never found her body, although you know from the files we concluded that she was drowned or left in somewhere no one would find her. And, I could never quite see Parch as a murderer. He obviously didn't want her testimony to be used to put him away for years, but it wasn't like he was going to get life – or anything like it – for embezzlement. So, it's hard to see the motive for killing your friend."

"Or having her killed?"

"That's even more risky. Once you involve an accomplice, they might turn on you. Happens more than you might think."

"But somebody had a motive to get rid of her," Zora said with just a hint of belligerence in her voice. The question was bothering her, too, and now she was disappointed that Detective Pete Le Gall didn't seem to have any new ideas on this subject or even want to share anything that could be helpful.

"Motives come from different places," he told her, putting down his cup. You could assume someone wanted to silence Ms. Hubbard, probably Parch. But motives can be built around disputes over money, jealousy, revenge, fear and sometimes just plain hatred."

Zora looked at him steadily as she absorbed this. "If any of those were motives for whoever killed Jane, I can't imagine who the killer was. But maybe I have to start rethinking the people she knew. And there are more of them for me to see."

Le Gall frowned and exhaled loudly, which sounded to Zora like a sound of exasperation. "Who are planning to contact next?"

"I want to meet the woman Parch swindled in Denver. And I want to meet with Jane's second cousin and anyone else she was close to at the school where we both taught. I've also gotten some information that Jane may have had a brief romance when she was getting her master's degree in Illinois. The man may have been married. I don't even have a name at this point. But if he had a jealous wife, I guess it's possible that there's a motive for murder buried in the past." She did not tell him that she had at least two other visits she was determined to make, to each of the Parches. That could wait.

Pete gazed past her at a painting over her head. "Don't ever discount how many years some people can hold grudges. We had a case once where a wife killed her ex-husband thirty years after their divorce because she could never get over the fact that he had thrown out all her mother's china dishes!"

Zora gave him a small smile. "But at least you solved that one!"

Pete looked up at her soberly and nodded. She realized that her comment might have sounded like a criticism of his work on Jane's case, so she added, "And I just have a feeling that with all the work you and your colleagues did about Jane that there will be an answer about what happened to her, too."

"I doubt it. We followed the leads we had, and I spent a lot of time for several years looking for new ones." His tone seemed clearly defensive. But he continued, "Sometimes with cold cases, the killer or killers get over confident after time has gone by. You can email me or call if you find anything you think would be pertinent." He signaled for the check, and Zora realized she was not likely to get any more information from him. "But it's clear he wants me to communicate with him, first, rather than go back to the Columbus police if I do find out anything," she told herself. "So maybe, just maybe, he's beginning to doubt that they left some stone unturned?" It gave her a ray of hope.

Zora handed him her card as they got up to leave. He pulled out his wallet and gave her one of his, which, she noted showed him as "Detective First Class, retired." She felt a pang of regret that the conversation had been so impersonal – nearly hostile. She liked this retired detective but knew that he must be feeling something like embarrassment that this unknown woman, who was clearly an amateur, was pursuing something that in his professional life remained virtually unsolved. She tried one more thing.

"I know you met son Roy some years ago and that you talked recently. If you ever make it to Boston, I know Roy would be happy to see you." She paused. "And I appreciate your meeting with me today." He held out his hand, and this time his grip seemed a little firmer. They parted in the parking lot. On the way to the airport, the traffic was light, giving Zora a few moments to reflect that Peter Le Gall seemed almost indifferent to her quest to find what happened to Jane. "But the one time he almost smiled, I liked him better," she aid to herself – even if he didn't have any new clues for her in her search for Jane Hubbard.

* * *

"What are you going to do next?" Ellie put down her coffee cup and eyed the frosted pumpkin bars Zora was offering. Surely one wouldn't hurt? They were sitting in Zora's living room in Cambridge, discussing Zora's Columbus trip.

"I've made a list of people to see. I'm saving Parch 'til last – if I see him at all. I did some research – he's alive and has moved from Florida into some kind of place, assisted living, I guess, in Virginia. I found out where his ex-wife is and I'm going to visit her in Florida – if she'll see me. I've made arrangements to talk to the woman in Denver who didn't press charges against Parch. And I plan to visit Jane's second cousin. But now I'm wondering if there is any point in tackling this story about Jane's having had an affair in graduate school. Hard to believe it could have mattered so many years later, but maybe there was a jealous wife."

Ellie took the first bite of pumpkin. "This is really good, Zora! One of your own recipes?"

Zora smiled. "No, straight out of the *Boston Globe* food section. Rashad always liked them. Glad you do, too."

"Do you have a theory yet? Is it possible that maybe Jane got injured somehow and ended up in some kind of facility and nobody has known about here all these years?"

Zora finished her own coffee. "I don't think so. The Columbus police were very thorough. They not only checked on all the hospitals and other facilities like nursing homes in Columbus but they checked in all the other major Ohio cities, too. And they went back after several months to see if any unidentified person had turned up. No results. Jane had friends at Ohio University in Athens, and they checked especially closely there. It's like she vanished into thin air. The lead detective – he's retired now – wrote in the record that they thinks her body was disposed of either in some kind of water – although they dragged several rivers – or buried somewhere no one has ever found. Maybe at a construction site. I tend to believe him."

"Tyler and I don't like the idea of your seeing Parch. He could be dangerous if he killed her and thinks someone is going to be able to prove that finally. Would the police maybe interview him again?"

"I'm not going to see him yet. And I'll talk with you and clear it with Roy if I do. Don't worry. I'm not going to do anything foolish."

"Maybe I can come with you on some of these visits? I have almost the whole summer off from teaching, my book is at the publisher's, and my on-line materials for next semester are in good shape. Tyler has so many meetings and conferences to attend, I'm not sure he would know I'm gone!"

"Oh, I think he'd know." Zora reached over and squeezed her younger friend's hand. "He's very lucky to have you – and he knows it."

"Well, just let me know how I – we – can help. I owe you that."

Zora got up to retrieve the coffee pot. As she poured for them, she had a thought. "You don't 'owe' me anything, but maybe there is something you can do – or, really Tyler, if he's willing. I don't know anything about this supposed affair Jane had – not who it was with, not anything about the man. But if I could find out more from Phyllis, maybe Tyler could find out from people at the University of Illinois if anyone there knows anything or remembers anything about Jane. I know it's a long shot, and I'm a little embarrassed to ask Tyler for something like this. Does he know the president there? Do you think this is crazy?"

Ellie's eyes sparkled. "I think Tyler would love to play sleuth. And, yes, he's friends with the U of I president – they were actually in grad school together years ago. Tyler would do anything for you. I'll ask him tonight."

"Let me know what he says. I'll try to get some more information from Phyllis so Tyler has something to go on. Meanwhile, I'm probably going to visit Denver next. I'm not sure that will produce much, either, but it may fill in some gaps at least about Parch. If, in the end, I can prove he did it, they might throw him back in prison. At least I hope so."

CHAPTER SEVEN

Two weeks later, Zora found herself picking up a rental car from Denver International Airport. Her next stop was Lakewood.

While standing in the reception area of Carter-by-the-Lake, Zora tilted her head back, squinted and looked up at the vaulted, crimson painted ceiling. Reluctantly, she reached into her purse and took out what she called her "walking around glasses". With them on, she could see more clearly – the ceiling had tiny, chain-link patterns in gold. "Pretentious," she thought.

"Would you like to sit down? Mrs. St. George will be down shortly." The receptionist smiled at Zora, who nodded as she surveyed the options – she hated things that she could fall in to. A small sofa looked safe, and she sat down gingerly. "Good back support," she observed approvingly. Generally, she liked the spaciousness of this meeting area and the building itself, "but probably expensive" she said to herself. Places like this that moved you from independent living to assisted living and then (if you needed it) to nursing care were all over in the Boston area, too. "So, I suppose I'll be in a place like this one of these days," Zora thought, "but not yet."

The elevator in the north corner of the big room opened and a wheel chair emerged, carrying a surprisingly robust looking woman with pink cheeks and white hair, whom Zora thought looked younger than her 80 years. She was dressed in a long, black skirt of fine wool and a red jacket. Zora stood up and marched over to the slowly moving wheelchair. She held out her hand. "Good morning! I'm Zora Erickson – are you Mrs. St. George?"

The woman in the wheelchair grasped its arms as if to try to stand and then gave up the effort. "Yes. Please tell me again who you are and why you are here."

Zora was prepared for this. When she wrote to Germaine St. George, she carefully explained that she was trying to solve the disappearance of an old friend and that Mrs. St. George might be able to give her valuable information – but she had not mentioned Jane's name, nor Murray Parch's. The reply – a letter – had come not from Germaine but from the administrator of Carter, saying that Mrs. St. George would be pleased to meet with Mrs. Erickson if a date and time could be arranged.

"Please call me Zora. My last name is Erickson. It is very good of you to see me. I hope you won't mind my telling you a little story to explain why I am here."

The other woman nodded her head, not saying anything but looking intently at Zora, who noticed that she wore hearing aids in both ears.

"I am a retired art teacher," Zora began, deciding to keep it simple. "I had a friend, an English teacher, back in Dublin, Ohio, some years ago. I left Dublin for Boston when I was still young, but we kept up with each other. My friend retired when she was sixty-two and then shortly after that, she disappeared. No one ever found her or knew what happened to her. She has been missing for almost thirteen years. Her name is Jane Hubbard.

Zora sat back and watched St. George's face closely. No reaction except a pleasant, rather vague stare. The pause was so long that Zora wondered if the older woman had heard her.

Then: "What's it like outside? Is it warm?"

Zora hesitated. "Yes, it's fine. I didn't even wear a sweater."

"Let's go out," and with that, Germaine started wheeling herself toward the front door. Zora, surprised, got up and followed, holding the door open.

Germaine continued pushing her wheelchair until they were several yards from the building. She turned down a path lined with pink Knockout roses. Zora could see a corner of the lake. "You could sit there," the older woman said, pointing to a stone bench. More of a command than an invitation, Zora thought as she sat down, pleased to find the bench more comfortable than she anticipated.

"So, you want to know if he ever said anything about her. If I knew about her. Is that it? Maybe if I think he killed her?" This time, it was Germaine who was looking intently at Zora. Whatever Zora expected before their meeting, this wasn't it!

"Mrs. St. George, can we start over? If you are referring to Murray Parch, I do know that you filed charges against him and then dropped them. That is none of my business. I do know that he was later convicted of swindling my friend, Jane Hubbard, and another person in Columbus, Ohio." Zora moved over on the bench so that she was looking directly at Germaine.

"What I don't know are a great many things. What I *do* know is that after all these years, no one is looking for Jane. I was one of her closest friends. I'm retired, I have time on my hands, and I have a guilty conscience because I have done nothing – nothing – to try to find her. Until now. My son is a detective and he has given me some guidance. I would like to find out what happened to Jane. I believe I owe her that. So, I'm talking with people who may be able to help me, even if they don't know they can. When I found out about you, I thought you might be one of them."

There was a short silence. Zora had planned her next move. She opened her purse and took out the last photograph she had of Jane. It was the glossy print, still in good shape, showing Jane sitting on the bench near the unnamed body of water. She handed it to Germaine. "This was Jane."

The older woman stared at the picture and then slowly took it in both hands, studying it. After a moment, she handed it back to Zora, turned her head away and looked down the path. She did not move her wheelchair. When she turned her head back, Zora could not read the look in her eyes.

"I never met your friend, Jane, but, yes, I know who she was. I followed the case in the papers. I was sorry to read that she went missing." She paused. Zora did not know whether to ask a question or let the conversation unfold on its own. She decided to wait.

"He got away with two hundred thousand of my money – a little more than that, actually. My husband, Frank, died two years before I met Murray. I thought I could manage our money myself. I met him at a party, and I liked what he had to say. He had other clients, he told me, especially back in Ohio. He gave me names. I didn't bother to check with them. He came to our house – I was living in Arvada then, in a big house my husband and I built twenty years earlier. I loved that house." She frowned a little, looking around the path and off toward the lake, as if to say "better than here."

She sat silent for a few minutes, her eyes closing, then opening, not looking at Zora. Instead, she seemed to be focusing on the lake, which threw off shimmers of light in the last morning sun. Finally, she turned again toward Zora.

"At first, I saw dividends coming into my account, so I didn't suspect anything. Murray was always very attentive, very good to me. He would come to see me, buy me cigarettes, take me to lunch, answer my phone calls. But two years later, when I asked a friend of mine, an accountant, to help me with taxes, she figured out what was wrong – that the reports were doctored and the shares were being sold off. When I confronted him, he denied it, of course. Said she misunderstood my accounts. She offered to get me a lawyer, but my late husband had a friend who did legal work for us, so I called him. I was angry and embarrassed. At first, I didn't want to file charges, but he insisted that was the right way. So I let him file."

Germaine reached into the pocket of her jacket and took out a delicate, white embroidered handkerchief. She dabbed at the corner of her left eye and replaced the small square in her pocket. Zora wondered if, after all this time, Parch's deception was still an emotional subject with her. "Probably would be for me if I were the victim!" she thought.

"Two weeks after charges were brought, Murray came to me. He sat in my living room and literally cried. He said he had meant to replace my money, that he had medical needs. He had told me once that his wife was back in Ohio, that they were separated. I never really knew anything more about her, but I imagined that the medical needs were hers. He asked me to give him time, that he would report to me every few weeks what he was doing and how much of my money he had put back. I remember asking him if he was doing this to anybody else, any of his other clients, and he said, 'no, absolutely not.'"

Zora hesitated. "Why did you believe he was only cheating you and not any of his other clients?"

"I don't know that he wasn't! They may have been too embarrassed to come forward. But with me, I think he thought he could get away with it because I trusted him." Germaine paused again, and looked at a rose blossom a few inches from her left hand. She reached out to stroke the rose.

"Anyway, I dropped the charges. My lawyer was furious, and my accountant friend wasn't happy with me, either. But in a way, I still trusted Murray."

"Then what happened?"

"Two weeks later when I hadn't heard from him, I called his office. The number was disconnected. I never before called him at home, but I tried that, too. He didn't have a mobile phone, or if he did, he never gave me that number. I went down to the office building. There were people painting the office. Someone told me the business that had been there had moved to Columbus, Ohio."

She paused again, as if trying to find words to explain. "And, of course, I never saw any of my money. Fortunately, I have other income. I did feel that maintaining our big house was an extravagance, so I sold it. That left me more than enough to move in here." She paused. She was no longer stroking the rose. Instead, she tore off a petal and dropped it to the ground.

"When did you learn about Jane?"

"Right after Murray moved back to Ohio, I subscribed to the *Columbus Dispatch*. It came in the mail, every day, a day or two late. I wanted to see what he was up to there. I didn't know how to use the Internet in those days. Your friend's name was one of the people he had mentioned as a client when I first met him. I never tried to call or get in touch with her." Germaine turned away from Zora again and stared at the path leading to the lake. Her hands lay still in her lap. A crow landed in the oak across from them. She ignored its raucous call.

"I didn't read anything about him – or about her – until some months later. I think it was in the winter. Anyway, it said he was under indictment for swindling two clients. Your friend was one."

"Was he still in contact with you then?" Zora realized her questions must be painful for Germaine, but she was here to help Jane, not to make someone else feel better.

"I had one letter from him, shortly after he moved back. He asked for time to replace my money." She paused; Zora waited.

"I wrote him back that I expected him to keep his bargain and replace the money. I didn't give him a deadline – what was the point? Then, I didn't hear from him again and I finally read about the indictment."

"Did you consult your lawyer then?"

"No, why would I? Murray wasn't going to repay me. He was already in enough trouble. He obviously didn't have the money."

"And when did you learn about Jane's disappearance?"

"Right after it happened, I guess. I was still getting the *Dispatch*. It reported that she was declared missing – something about her car being found somewhere not near where she lived."

"Did you do anything after you read that?"

"No, there was nothing I knew and nothing that I could do to help."

"Was "I read what the judge said when he sentenced Murray. That he thought evidence suggested Murray was responsible for Jane Hubbard's disappearance so he would give him the maximum sentence, even though no one could prove it. I thought it was a strange thing for a judge to say – and he later went on to become the state's Supreme Court's Chief Justice, I think."

"Yes, he did," Zora said dryly. "I guess you know that the other person whom he swindled in Ohio was a woman who died before the trial. She may have committed suicide. So, Jane would have been the only person who could have provided evidence against Parch." She paused, looking closely at Germaine again for any re-action. She saw none. Hands still folded in the lap. Slight frown. "And that's why I am trying to find out if there is any connection between Jane's disappearance and the case involving Mr. Parch. If even the judge at this trial felt there was a probable connection, I want to see if this is a blind path – or if the police simply didn't do their work."

Germaine moved her head slightly and looked appraisingly at Zora. "You really liked her, didn't you? You must miss her."

Zora nodded, surprised by the lump forming in her throat. "Yes, and I'm angry, too. Angry that no one seems to care. I owe this to her."

"Do you have children?" Germaine's voice went up a few notes. She drew her wheelchair an inch or two closer to the bench.

"Yes, two, both with families. My son lives near me, so I see them often. My daughter is in Atlanta."

"We never had children. My husband was fifteen years older than I was and he had a busy career running his own company. I have a niece and a nephew, though. They come to see me."

Zora didn't know why Germaine changed the subject, and she wasn't sure how to get back to questions about Jane. She saw Germaine shiver slightly. "Are you cold? Do you want to go inside?"

"Yes. I get chilled easily. Ever since my stroke five years ago, I don't seem to have the stamina I did once. I used to play tennis and golf, and I liked to go on walking trips. Not now. I had to move from independent living to what they call here 'assisted living'. Means you need care but you're not yet an invalid or senile."

"Here, let me push you," Zora offered, getting up off the bench. Her own back felt a bit stiff .

"Thank you," Germaine answered and was silent as they started down the path. Then, "Did you drive here?"

Zora stopped pushing the chair. "I flew into the Denver airport and rented a car."

"Could we go for a ride? I don't get out often."

Zora changed direction and began pushing the wheelchair toward the parking lot. Her rental sat in the front row, a silver Corolla. She felt glad of the chance to continue the conversation but wasn't sure she could get Germaine into the front seat. When they got there, however, Germaine raised herself up from the wheelchair and pivoted into the passenger seat with more strength than Zora thought she might have. "Just leave the chair here, over there on the grass. People do that all the time. We won't be gone all that long, I suppose."

After Zora started the car, she turned to Germaine. "Is there anywhere special you would like to go?"

"We can drive down by the lake. I'll show you the way. It's nice there on sunny days. Sometimes they have picnics down there for us."

A five minute drive took them to a parking area that overlooked the man-made lake. To Zora's surprise, the older woman opened the car door and breathed deeply as the warm air seeped into the car. "There used to be row boats down here. Not sure what they've done with them. I grew up on a lake in Minnesota. In those days, I could row all day. Do you like the water?"

Zora smiled. "Actually, I'm a little bit afraid of large bodies of water. I guess that's because I never learned about boating. My son wants me to take a cruise with him and his wife. I'm resisting. Did you and your husband cruise?"

Germaine shook her head. "Too busy. He always seemed to be too busy with work. We talked about doing things like that, but then he died."

They sat for a time without talking. Finally, Germaine closed her door. "Let's go back. Thank you for bringing me here." She paused. "The one thing I don't want to do is to die in this place as an invalid.

As long as I can get out a little, I'm fine. But if I get any worse off than I am now, I think I would push my wheelchair down here and just keep going.

Zora assumed she meant "into the lake". She had no easy rejoinder for this and so stayed silent as she started the car. She, too, didn't want to die old, useless and helpless. "Concentrate on what you are doing now," she told herself as they pulled into the Carter parking lot.

In few minutes, she had Germaine out and in her wheelchair and was pushing her into the building. They reached the reception desk. "I'll say good-by here," she offered, extending her hand. The other woman took it and held it for a moment. "Thank you for coming. I hope you find out about your friend." She turned the wheelchair toward the elevator. Zora watched until the door closed.

Zora got back in the Corolla and immediately noticed something white on the passenger side floor. She bent over to pick it up. It was the embroidered handkerchief Germaine St. George had used when they were sitting outside. Zora cut the engine and got out of the car. At the front desk, she explained what had happened. "I'll just leave this with you," she told the pleasant receptionist.

"Oh, you can take it up to Mrs. St. George's room if you like. I'm sure she'll appreciate it. She's in room L-446. When you get to the fourth floor, take the L wing." Zora suddenly thought that she might like to see Germaine's living quarters.

When she got to L-446, the door was ajar. Zora hesitated and then knocked. "Come in!" a voice said. Zora pushed the door open.

Germaine was sitting by the window on the far side of what looked to be a tastefully decorated small living room. Blue curtains, pulled back with a sash, a coffee table, chairs in gold brocade. A credenza holding books and framed pictures. A short hallway off to the left, leading to what looked like a spacious bedroom, which revealed the corner of an unmade bed and a dresser. When the older woman turned her wheelchair and saw Zora, she looked startled. Zora caught the look. "I'm so sorry to barge in on you but the receptionist suggested I bring this up myself. You dropped it in the car." She held out the white handkerchief. Germaine moved her wheelchair across the room. She pushed closed the door to the hallway. "Thank you," she said. "It's precious to me – it was a gift."

"Glad I found it then," Zora replied. Clearly, she wasn't going to be invited in for tea! "I must be going. I have other appointments today. It was good of you to see me." She took as much time as she could to look around the room. She saw nothing of consequence. As she left, she realized Germaine was watching her walk down the hallway.

As she left the grounds of Carter-by-the-Lake, Zora wondered if her next visit was going to be a complete waste of time. She had made the appointment when she wasn't sure she would be able to meet with Germaine St. George. Now she had, and nothing had come of it. So why would visiting her late husband's company prove any more enlightening? However, a vice president was going to meet with her, and she intended to keep the appointment.

CHAPTER EIGHT

Link Controls occupied two buildings in Englewood, not far from downtown Denver. Zora looked at her watch. Almost 3 p.m. Time to go in at the building marked "headquarters". She introduced herself at the front desk and was directed to a conference room on the first floor. Everything in this building looked new, and she wondered if the company, which made heating and air conditioning equipment, had always been in this location. She guessed not.

"Mrs. Erickson - I'm so sorry not to have met you at the desk!" A tall, willowy young man with long, blond hair exclaimed, as he rushed into the conference room. He reached for Zora's hand and shook it vigorously. "I'm Ed Whalen. Please sit down. I just read your letter over again. It's quite a story although I'm not sure quite how I can help you."

Zora looked around the conference room. Long, beautifully polished rosewood table and scarlet leather chairs. A table at the back with a large water dispenser, plus coffee and tea making equipment. Windows with beige vertical shades. Pictures on the wall, all with name plates. One larger than the others and the name plate easy to read even without her glasses: "Franklin St. George, Founder." She moved over to the wall to look at it more closely. Ed followed her. "Yes, that's Frank. He started the company almost fifty years ago. I never knew him, of course. I've been here ten years and Frank died before I came, but my father worked for him. That's why they gave me your letter when you asked to see someone. Shall we sit down?"

Zora took the nearest chair. "Mr. Whalen, thank you for seeing me. I will try to be brief. Since you know my story, or rather I should say Jane's story, then let me just say that I am trying to follow up on any information that might be significant in finding Jane." He nodded and smiled – and waited.

"When I found out that Mrs. St. George was swindled by the same man - Murray Parch - who deceived Jane, I thought that perhaps I should learn more about what he did out here. I've seen Mrs. St. George earlier today. She was quite frank about her business involvement with Parch, but I didn't really learn anything that would seem to bear on Jane's case." While she was speaking, she noticed that several emotions played over Ed Whalen's face – curiosity, sympathy, puzzlement, sadness. What a nice young man, she thought! Either that, or he's a good actor. "However, since I'm here and you are being kind enough to see me, perhaps you can tell me about Mr. St. George."

"Of course, if I can. My father used to talk about him. He liked him. Everybody, including Dad, used to say that Frank St. George worked harder than anyone else in the company. You know, Link didn't make much money at first. Guess he put in the long hours to make it successful. Dad used to say Frank didn't have any hobbies. No children, either, as far as I know. But he was good to the people who worked here. Profit sharing, real pensions. He invested a lot of his own money in the company."

"Did your father ever talk about Germaine St. George – or meet her?"

"I don't remember anything specific but he would have known her. There were parties. The company gives an annual Christmas party. And we've always had a summer picnic." A smile brightened his already animated face. "Maybe I can find some pictures – would you like to see them? We have an archivist. If she's in, maybe I can get an album or two – or a CD. Do you mind waiting here a few minutes? Would you like tea or coffee – or ice tea? Water? We have everything!"

"Water would be very nice, thank you." He poured her a glass, with ice, before leaving the room. Zora got up to look at more of the portraits hanging on the walls. Past vice presidents, past board members. Only one woman, who was identified as "comptroller" in the first years of the company. Franklin St. George's photograph was formal – suit and tie, solemn look. She thought she remembered seeing a smaller version of it on Germaine's credenza in her living room.

Ed Whalen returned with two photo albums under his arm. "Not digitized yet but here they are – pictures from the early days!" He laid the albums on the table and opened the first one. The photos were clearly from a Christmas party. Someone had meticulously labeled each picture with the date and location. Zora took out her reading glasses. Ed looked over her shoulder. "See, that's Frank. St. George, there, in the middle. I guess that's Mrs. St. George next to him."

Zora gazed at the woman in the photo. She was obviously younger than her husband. Medium height, striking, curly brown hair, piled on top of her head. A blue dress with a discreet neckline that, nevertheless, showed off high breasts. She was smiling and holding a glass of what looked like champagne. Zora turned the page. More Christmas party pictures. Then, pictures from some outdoor event – probably the annual picnic. Ed pointed – "That's him, in the blue shirt." Most of the men in the picture wore Bermuda shorts, but not St. George. No evidence of his wife. Then, on the next page, she appeared. Dressed in a short tennis skirt, she was laughing with another woman on the edge of a tennis court surrounded by flowers. The caption under the picture gave the date and read "Germaine St. George celebrating the doubles championship with her partner at the Leland Country Club."

Half to herself, Zora said, "she told me she used to play tennis – and golf. But you said her husband didn't?"

"Well, maybe he did sometimes but I know Dad always said people in the company thought Mr. St. George should get a hobby."

Zora leafed through more pages and turned to the second album. More of the same – parties, events, some pictures of St. George without his wife, some pictures with her, and a few more of her celebrating a tennis championship at the Leland Country Club.

"May I borrow one of these pictures for a few days?"

"Sure! You can just mail it back later. Which one would you like?" Obviously Ed was curious, but he did not ask any questions.

Zora picked one of the tennis pictures, judging from the date that Germaine would have been about fifty-five, her female partner somewhat younger. She put it carefully in her purse. "This has been very helpful, Mr. Whalen, and I won't take up any more of your time. If I do need to talk with you again, may I have your business card?"

"Sure!" He dug into his pocket and extracted a single card. "And I have your address and phone number from your letter."

Zora opened her purse again and tucked in his card. "I promise to return this picture."

When they reached the front door of the building, Ed Whalen shook her hand vigorously. "I hope you find out what happened to your friend. You let me know if we can be of any help here. And please let me know what you find out when it's all solved!"

"I will, and thank you," Zora replied, thinking that he showed more confidence in her abilities than she, herself, felt at the moment.

In the parking lot, she looked at her watch. Almost 4 p.m. Would a country club be open now? Certainly! It was a lovely day, the tennis courts and the golf course would probably be full, and if the place had a bar, as it undoubtedly did, this might be the best time to do what she now had in mind. She got in her car, looked up "Leland Country Club" on her phone and programmed in the location. The drive would only take fifteen minutes, depending on traffic. She started out.

Zora turned at the sign, "Leland Country Club – Members Only" and drove toward the large, white neo-Colonial clubhouse. She saw the pro shop off to the left but elected to try the main building first. Inside, instead of a receptionist, she found a spaghetti board listing the events of the day, with arrows indicating the direction of the restaurant, bar, and meeting rooms. She turned right and followed the corridor in a sweeping turn until she found herself at the entrance of a cozy, oak-paneled room with an excellent view of the golf course.

Comfortable tables and chairs dotted the heavily carpeted space. Two parties of men and two women in tennis shorts were drinking, eating and visiting. Along the left wall was a short bar with stools. The only man sitting there seemed to be in deep conversation with the bar tender, who was wiping glasses and talking at the same time. Zora went up to the end of the bar and pulled out a stool. Both men stopped their conversation, looked at her, and smiled. Zora realized that they must wonder what an elderly black lady in a business suit and high heels was doing at their bar. Obviously, she had not just come from the golf course or the tennis courts.

The bar tender left his male customer and came toward her. His name tag read "Tony". "Hi! What can I get for you?"

"A glass of Merlot, thank you."

"You got it!" The drink was in front of her in less than a minute. "How about some peanuts?"

"Fine," Zora replied and looked around. Other than the original bar stool occupant, she doubted anyone else in the room could hear her. She took a sip of her wine – "nicely chilled" – and took the photograph of Germaine St. George out of her purse. When the peanuts arrived, Zora asked "Do you have a minute?" The bar tender glanced around. "Sure, what can I do you for?"

"I'm from Boston, and I'm visiting Denver to try to find something for a friend of mine. I'm wondering if you recognize this photograph." She slid the picture across the top of the bar. "I believe this taller lady was a member here at one time."

Tony pulled out a pair of reading glasses and squinted at the picture. "No, I don't recognize her and that snapshot looks old. I've been here six years, so maybe this was before my time." Zora had guessed as much. But as she hoped, the older man who was sitting two bar stools away was listening to the conversation. He got up and moved next to her. She left the photograph on the bar.

"Mind if I look?" he asked. "Name's Al Romundstad. Been a member here for forty years. Which gal are you asking about?"

"The taller one with the curly hair." Zora pointed to Germaine.

Al either didn't use glasses or didn't have them with him. He brought the picture close to his face. Then he handed it back to Zora with a broad smile. "Sure, that can't be anyone but Germaine St. George. Crack tennis player, she was. Won a lot of tournaments. Husband owned a company out here. Used to see her a lot, him less. Don't think he was ever on the courts. Might have golfed, but I don't recall that. Nice enough fellow. She was good looking!"

Zora expected that Al would ask what she was trying to find out – but he didn't, so she continued. "I know her husband died some time ago. Do you remember if she continued coming to the club after that?"

Al looked around for his drink just as Tony silently handed him a fresh glass. Highland single malt, Zora saw as Tony replaced the bottle. Rashad had liked Scotch.

"Oh, she was a regular even after that." Al took a sip of his Scotch and smiled at the glass. "Had lots of women friends and played with some of the men, too. She was good. Brought her boyfriend here a few times that I saw, but that was a long time ago."

"I see," Zora paused. "Did she marry this 'boy friend'?"

Al laughed and took a long sip of his Scotch. "Not that I know of, and I think I would've heard. He was younger than she was. Don't know if it was a serious thing, but he was a good looking enough guy. Talked up the members about money, investments. I remember that. Outgoing. Probably more fun than old Frank." He took another sip and now looked directly at Zora. "You here about something to do with the St. Georges?"

She had anticipated this. "I lost a good friend some years ago. I'm trying to fill in some gaps in her life, her last few months. For her family. We think she spent some time in Denver. The St. Georges apparently knew her."

The weak logic of this explanation did not seem to disturb her fellow drinker. "Well, I expect you can just look up old Germaine on the net and find out where she is. Seems to me I heard she went to a home or someplace like that out here. Want me to ask around?" Al was eyeing his almost empty glass. Tony was serving a new table of three.

"No, that's fine and I appreciate your offer. I'll find her." Zora picked up her bill, opened her purse and took out cash, being careful to leave a generous tip. She stood up.

"Very nice to have met you, Mr. Romundstad. You have good taste in Scotch. That was my husband's favorite, too."

He answered her with a smile and held out his hand. "Hope you find out about your friend."

Zora left before he could ask her any more questions. There were some she wanted to ask him, but she needed to collect her thoughts before she went any further down this particular path. "A boyfriend?" she said to herself as she walked to the car.

And now she was remembering the glimpse she had earlier into Germaine's bedroom when she returned the handkerchief. There was a picture frame on the side table by the bed. It was turned in such a way that Zora could only see that it looked like a photograph. She wished she could go back to Carter-by-the-Lake for another look, but of course, that was impossible.

"But if that is Murray on her dresser, what isn't she telling me about their relationship? And if they stayed in touch, what does she really know about Jane?" If she couldn't ask Germaine St.

George directly, she was going to have to find another way to un-cover the information. Zora started her car and drove slowly down the country club drive. Her return flight to Boston would leave the next morning. "I think I'm going to have to come back here," she decided, but even as she thought about it, she didn't know what she should be looking for, and that bothered her.

It wasn't until after dinner at a small Mexican restaurant and as she was relaxing in her hotel room that she saw the email from Phyllis. It read, simply "Call me – I may have remembered some-thing". Glancing at the time – well after dinner in Columbus – she dialed Phyllis. "I hope she's up," Zora thought just as she heard Phyllis' voice. "I'm in Denver," Zora explained, so sorry for calling you so late." Phyllis laughed. "It's 'Antiques Road Show' night so, of course, I'm still up."

Then her voice became serious. "Zora, when you were here I told you I never heard Jane mention the name of this professor she was involved with. But I thought about it after our conversa-tion and remembered something. One time Jane and I visited the Fine Arts Museum for a visiting show of Picasso – something like 'Picasso through the Ages', I think. There was a particularly love-ly painting of a reclining woman from his 'blue' period. I had nev-er seen it before. We both read the notes under the painting, and then Jane said very softly, almost as if to herself, "Jamie would have liked that". I didn't ask who 'Jamie' was – and it could have been a student, or former student or just a friend. Sometimes 'Jamie' is a girl's name, too, you know? But she might have meant her profes-sor friend from Illinois. I'm sorry I didn't think of it to tell you ear-lier. And it may mean nothing."

Zora thanked her friend warmly. Even while she was listening to Phyllis, a tingle went up her arms, a sure sign to her that some-thing important was about to happen. At any rate, now she had one part of one name. She could share this with Ellie, and ask her to tell Tyler. Maybe it would help.

It was late, but she decided to send a note to Pete Le Gall. She knew that he probably still resented her trying to reopen the case. But she felt that he was perhaps the only ally she had, even if a reluctant one. Besides, what harm could it do? In her email, she summarized her visit to Germaine, briefly mentioning the picture by Germaine's bed that was not visible, adding "I don't think I've found out anything new here but something tells me there is more to find out." She closed by adding: "Jane's friend, Phyllis called me. She thinks she heard Jane once mention the first name of her 'friend' – maybe the one she had the affair with at the university. Phyllis remembers it as 'Jamie', but not anything more. Heading back to Boston tomorrow."

CHAPTER NINE

Zora was determined to keep to her schedule, which meant traveling again a week after Denver, but this next visit was not one she relished.

Rain began to pelt her windshield just as Zora reached Sebring. Her navigation system showed three miles to the Holiday Inn, and she lowered her speed to match the city speed limit. The weather made her feel jumpy, but she knew the real reason was her uncertainty about this whole trip. "I wonder if I should have called her first after all," she thought for the hundredth time. For all she knew, Mai might slam the door in her face. "And if that happens, I guess I will just have to enjoy the Florida sunshine," Zora said to herself, noting that the rain was coming down harder than ever. She had read somewhere that these brief storms were typical summer occurrences in central Florida.

Instead of going straight to her motel, she decided to look up Mai Parch. The Google map had displayed her house in a development on the east side of town. Finding it proved easy. The small houses looked similar except for their varying shades of pastel. Mai's was a dark shade of pink. Zora pulled up to the curb next to a thin strip of grass, on the other side of which was a sidewalk that led to the house. She meant to stay just for a minute or two, looking at the house, but the rain now began streaking horizontally and she could barely see beyond the car's hood. Two minutes went by with no let up. Then, just as the pelting began to lessen, at the passenger side window someone appeared, all but obscured by a large, black umbrella. Whoever it was tapped on the glass. Zora jumped but pressed the button to lower the window. She kept the engine running so she could pull out fast if she needed to.

Out from under the umbrella a small, neatly coifed head of black hair and glasses appeared. "Hello!" said a female voice, barely audible within the din of the still pouring rain. "You're from Methodist Hospital, aren't you! I'm Mai. I was expecting you tomorrow, but please come in. Let me come around to your side so you can get under my umbrella."

Too surprised to reply, Zora raised the passenger window, turned off the car's engine, and opened her door just as the small woman reached her with the umbrella. For a moment, she considered explaining right there that she wasn't whoever Mai was expecting, but then it struck her that perhaps this was divine guidance. She got out of the car, ducked under the umbrella and followed Mai into the house.

The first thing that struck Zora was how simply but artfully decorated the living room looked. One large, abstract painting with vivid colors and what could have been two horses hung on the far wall. Two red clay pottery vases with fresh flowers on a low table in front of a couch decorated in a blue patterned fabric. Two low chairs upholstered in eggshell white. The only unusual feature of the room was a desk ("maybe Danish modern?") with a matching computer table next to it. Mai was drawing up her desk chair to the sofa. "Please," she said gesturing toward Zora then the sofa. "I think you will be comfortable there."

Zora sat down, putting her purse on the floor beside her. She had no chance to turn on her smart phone recorder. She hoped she would be able to remember whatever came of this interview.

"Did you receive my report from last month? I made some suggestions this time. I think they could make the coding quicker."

Zora took a deep breath and sat forward. "Mrs. Parch, I am not from the hospital. I should have explained that to you outside. My name is Zora Erickson. I'm from Boston. I'm here because I am looking for someone, and I think you might be able to help me."

"You came all this way from Boston? Is it someone I know?"

"I'm not sure, and I want to apologize for not writing you or calling first. I really wasn't sure you would want to talk to me. The person I am looking for is probably dead, but she was a very close friend of mine. After all these years, I've realized that it is not right that no one knows what happened to her. Her name was Jane Hubbard."

Zora watched Mai closely. She saw a slight frown on the younger woman's brow but nothing more. Silence. Zora waited.

"I knew her. Yes. What is it you want from me?" The words sounded emotionless.

"You know she went missing, then. You know they never found her. I've read what the judge said at your husband – ex-husband's – sentencing. I'm not accusing him, Mrs. Parch. But I have the feeling someone who was involved with Jane must know something. Perhaps something they forgot to tell the police years ago. Perhaps something that seems irrelevant." She paused and looked closely at Mai. "Did you ever meet Jane?"

Mai stood up. "I am going to get water. May I bring you a glass?"

"That would be nice, yes," Zora answered quickly. Was this an excuse for Mai to think up some story? In less than a minute she reappeared with two cut crystal glasses – water with ice cubes. She put one down on a coaster in front of Zora but remained standing. She took a sip from her own glass and glanced toward her desk, as if searching for something.

"I knew her, yes. We invited her to our house. More than once. She had dinner with us. I thought she was a family friend." Mai put her own glass on the coffee table between them. She glanced around the room, as if expecting to see someone else. Then she turned back to Zora. "I may have been wrong. I have wondered about that for many years. I have thought that perhaps she was only *his* friend."

"Do you mean you think your husband and Jane were having an affair?" Zora hated asking this of someone who had probably suffered with an awful doubt for so long, but she was here to help Jane, not Mai Parch.

Mai sat down, arranging her skirt so no wrinkles showed. "He had other women. That was why I divorced him, you know. It wasn't just because of the money, because of what they accused him of – of defrauding those women. It was because he lied to me."

"I'm really sorry to cause you pain in bringing this all up," Zora said, wishing she could reach out with a gesture of sympathy, but this was not the time. "Did you ever have any idea that your husband was afraid of Jane, of how she might testify against him?"

Mai's gaze moved to her water glass. "No, I never heard him say anything like that. After he got away with taking money from that woman in Colorado, I expect he thought he could get away with anything. When your friend disappeared, he seemed upset.

But maybe that was an act. I don't know. After all this time, I don't know."

Zora felt sure she would not be welcome here much longer, but she had one more question that she really wanted to hear Mai answer.

"There was another person, another client of your husband's, who lost money with him. Julia Lefkowitz. Did you know her?"

This time, Mai looked up with a frown. "I heard him mention her, yes. But I don't think I ever met her. She committed suicide, didn't she?"

"That was the report at the time, yes."

"Are you saying you think she was murdered, too?"

Zora assumed the "too" implied that Mai thought – or knew – Jane was killed. "No, I'm not implying anything, but I understand that she was a client of his. Do you have any reason to think she was anything more?"

Mai got up. She walked over to her desk, picked up a CD case, put it down. Stayed at the desk, finally turned around. Her voice was low, unsteady. "I have told you. He had other women. I didn't ask who they were. I suppose I did not want to know. All I know was that he told lies, lies about where he was at times, lies about what he did. I was sure about that woman in Denver, but I know there were others. I found things. I didn't think your friend, Jane, was one of them, but I don't know that. I don't know if this Lefkowitz person was one of them or not. He told me he had a client who killed herself. I think he said she had mental problems, was unstable. Was that true?'

Zora had anticipated the question. "I didn't know Ms. Lefkowitz. She came along as a teacher at the high school in Dublin, where Jane and I both taught, but that was years after I left. I know they were very good friends. I know your husband became Julia's broker. I heard from other friends that she was a good teacher. If she had problems, I never heard. From pictures I have seen, she was beautiful." She paused, remembering the letter Jane had written about losing Julia. "Why people kill themselves we don't always know."

Mai said nothing but looked steadily at Zora, who felt the look was not one of animosity but perhaps only of sadness. Zora doubted she would learn much more here, but she had another question she knew she must ask.

"Mrs. Parch, before your husband went to prison – and I know you were separated then – did he ever tell you anything about Jane that he didn't at the time she disappeared?"

Mai picked up her nearly empty water glass, put it back down. "No, he told me nothing. Not then, not before. The last time he spoke about her that I remember, he said something like 'I hope they find out what happened to her'. Of course, after that, I realized she was someone who could testify against him. And if what they accused him of --- the fraud -- was true, she lost a lot of money because of him. So, maybe he killed her, or had her killed. That would have been his way, not to do it himself, not to get his hands dirty, but maybe to have it done."

Zora got up. If this woman knew anything more, it was not going to be revealed in this conversation. Zora's questions had caused pain. Maybe Mai knew more than she was telling, but she would have to decide on her own to share what she knew – if she knew something.

"Thank you, Mrs. Parch. I know this has not been easy, and I appreciated your seeing me. I will not keep you." Zora reached for her purse.

Unexpectedly, Mai got up and moved toward her. "Wait. I would like to give you my card. If you want to ask me anything else, maybe sometime later, you can call me. Or email. I am sorry about your friend. I always liked Jane. I did not want to see her to die." Mai held out a business card. Zora took it. "I have one, too, to give you." She reached into her purse. "And I appreciate your offer."

Mai looked closely at Zora for a moment. "Are you going to see him, too?" It was obvious who she meant. "I can give you his address."

Surprised, Zora nodded. "That would be helpful."

Mai went to her desk and wrote something swiftly on a small piece of paper. As she handed it to Zora, she said, "We don't talk, but every year on my birthday he sends me a card." She paused and looked out the window. The rain had stopped. "I don't send him anything."

Mai went to the front door and opened it. Warm, humid air filtered into the living room. As Zora moved past her to the porch, Mai said in a soft voice, "Perhaps one day you can tell me what you find out. I would like to know." Zora nodded.

As she got into her rental car, she saw Mai turn back into the house and close the door. Was she closing it on secrets that only she knew or was she as much in the dark about Jane as everyone else seemed to be? Zora simply did not know.

CHAPTER TEN

Back at her computer at home two days later, Zora began to assemble her notes. "I'll write this in two sections – like a diary, so I can remember where I was when, and then notes for each person I meet with." She was typing the details from the Chillicothe visit and the strange conversation with Mrs. Elijah when her landline phone rang. She saw that the call was from a university number. Expecting to hear Ellie's voice, she answered with "hello there"! "Hello, Zora," said the deep baritone voice, and she recognized Tyler Sheppard.

"Tyler! What a nice surprise! Did Ellie tell you I was back?

"Yes, and so am I. That is, from a very boring conference in San Francisco. But I may have learned something that could be helpful to you. And I would rather not share the information over the phone. Are you free for dinner tonight? Ellie is volunteering with the junior symphony association for its fund-raising gala, and has guaranteed she will not be home for dinner. She refused to prepare anything in advance for me, so it's either my own cooking or taking you to dinner."

Zora laughed. Tyler, himself, was a good cook. "Well, that's nice, but wouldn't you like to come here? I have lamb chops in the freezer and they could be thawed by dinner time!"

"If I can bring a bottle of wine, I will accept your gracious invitation. And dessert. I would like to bring dessert."

Zora knew what that meant – berries of some kind, lemon pound cake, Grand Marnier. Tyler's favorite dessert, according to Ellie.

"That's fine! What time is good for you?"

"Ah, the life of a university president goes on to all hours, but if I arrive between 6:30 and 7:00 p.m. will that accommodate you?"

"Perfectly. I will look for you then."

At 6:05 p.m., Zora saw Tyler's green BMW pull up to the curb. He climbed out, carrying two bags and walked up her stairs. She met him at the door.

Even with the bags in hand, he managed to give her a warm hug. Glancing at the townhouse next door – the one Ellie had lived in – he said, "I will never forget that porch. Or that night." Zora smiled. She knew how much he loved Ellie and how much he believed Zora was responsible for saving Ellie's life. She herself didn't quite look at it that way, but it was part of their personal myth now, and she had no wish to dispute it.

He helped open the wine – two bottles – a red blend for himself, Pino Grigio for her, and then they sat down in front of the cheese tray, crackers, and black olives. Tyler leaned back and let out a sigh. "He's aged a bit over this last year," Zora said to herself. Much as he loved what he did – and was good at it – she knew the job caused stress.

"How was your day?" she asked, as she supposed Ellie would ask him every night.

"It's still summer break, so I have a little more time to attend to things other than the day to day crises. We are doing well at fund raising. But it's constant. What I need is a rich, little old lady with no family, who adopts me or the university and leaves us all her money. So far, she has not turned up. So, I meet with alumni. Some of them are learning to be generous."

"Is that why you were on the West Coast?"

"Yes, partly, but also to attend a conference of university administrators. I didn't hear much of anything new, but I did learn something that may be useful for you."

He leaned forward. "Zora, I spent some time with Emile – he's my friend who heads the University of Illinois now – I think Ellie told you that."

Zora nodded.

"I told him the story about your friend Jane. I hope that wasn't a violation of your trust, but I felt he needed to know why I was asking questions."

Zora nodded again.

"We had drinks together on the first evening. What I told him was that your missing friend may have had a romantic relationship with one of her professors and that while it was a long shot, knowing who that was might help your investigation."

Tyler took a sip of his wine. "Good! I like this blend. Anyway, Emile was intrigued by the story about Jane and he made some phone calls and sent a message back to his staff assistant while we were at the conference. We were there for three days, and we had breakfast together the last morning. By then, he had information – and this is what he told me."

Zora put down her glass. She felt a slight tingle in her arms. Would there, finally, be some useful information?

"Assuming that your friend Jane did, in fact, have a romantic relationship with someone in the College of Education, there were three professors, or instructors, there at that time who had 'James' as part of their names. Of course, 'Jamie' could have been a nickname for someone whose real name was not 'James'. And, it may be that the man in question was not really a full-time professor but possibly a teaching assistant. Apparently the university's records don't show information on teaching assistants that far back."

Zora took another sip of wine and waited.

"There was one full professor whose name was James de Santos. He taught a course called 'Methods'. He would be 85 now, but he has been dead now for some six years. His widow, Leona, lives in Arizona. I have her contacts for you. Then, there was an Assistant Professor, named Carl James Armillato. He taught a course in philosophy of education. The university records show he retired and moved to Colorado - to Boulder - twenty years ago when he was 68, and he was apparently widowed some time after that. He is alive, and I have his address and a phone number for you, too. Finally, there was a Bradley James Mittdorf, who taught a course in early childhood education. He was killed in an automobile crash forty years ago, and there is no record of a surviving spouse."

Tyler reached into his jacket pocket and handed Zora a sheet of paper, neatly folded. "I don't know whether you will want to pursue any of this. Emile said he doubted there would be anyone still at the university or involved with the university community who would remember anything about a student-teacher affair from fifty-five or so years ago – if there even was one. I'm sorry I could not get more information for you, but it's been a long time."

Zora nodded, looking for a moment at the names. "I know it's unlikely that this will lead anywhere, but thank you very much. And please thank your friend, Emile."

Tyler smiled. "I think Emile was intrigued by the mystery. He asked that I let him know if you ever solved it. And he said that if he or the university could help in any other way, I should let him know."

They went to Zora's kitchen together, and after that they did not talk "business" for the rest of the evening.

CHAPTER ELEVEN

Pete Le Gall woke up on several nights after meeting Zora, wrestling with himself about whether it made any sense at all for him to reopen – even informally – the case of Jane Hubbard. Reopening a cold case was not something he relished, although he had participated in two others since his retirement and helped solve them. But lately, he was just glad to be done with active police work. Most of his best friends on the force were dead or retired, and some of the crime now was of an uglier kind than he ever dealt with. However, the Hubbard case had been his, and never really solved – no dead body, anyway. He admitted to himself that the Erickson woman seemed bright enough, and even though she was what he hated most in his professional life, an amateur detective, he had to admit that she might have turned up at least one piece of information they had all overlooked twelve years earlier, the witness Mrs. Elijah. He discounted anything about the Germaine person in Colorado. He wrestled with whether to call the new Columbus Chief of Police, Jess Murdock, who obviously knew that Zora Erickson was on a mission since her son had asked the Columbus police to send her the Hubbard file. In the end, Pete decided to visit Mrs. Elijah himself. "Then, if she really has anything useful to say, I can bring in someone on the force."

On the drive to Chillicothe, he mulled over how he would approach her. "If she was afraid of the police then, she isn't going to be happy to see me now." Of course, he was not in uniform, and even at his imposing height of six foot three he believed he could be gentle even persuasive. In his past life, he had interviewed victims, suspects, witnesses, even lawyers, and, usually, he got what he needed. By the time he arrived at St. Stephen's, he felt sure he could find a way to get Mrs. Elijah to talk.

But, as it turned out, she began the interrogation. After he parked in "visitors" at the home, he walked toward the front door. He wanted to take a few minutes to observe the place, so he sat down on one of the two facing iron wrought benches close to the entrance. Just then a dark-complexioned, slightly stooped over lady with a broom came out to the concrete entryway and began slowly sweeping up leaves and petals from the nearby trees. She didn't seem to notice him at first, but when she got within a couple of feet, she stopped and looked up. "What's your name?" She asked, sounding puzzled but not angry. He noticed that she was wearing a blue uniform that looked faded but clean.

"I'm Pete. Are you Mrs. Elijah? I'm a friend of Mrs. Erickson. Do you remember her?"

A frown. Then a look of recognition. "The Black lady? The one who came here to see about Miss Jane?"

"Yes. I am trying to help her. We still want to find Miss Jane, if we can."

She peered at him intently, backing up a step or two. "Are you from the police?"

He had anticipated the question. "Many years ago I was, but now I am retired and spend my time with my grandchildren. Except when I am trying to help a good friend, like Mrs. Erickson and her friend Miss Jane." The grandchildren story was a lie, but he hoped it would make him sound less threatening.

Abruptly, Mrs. Elijah laid her broom down and sat on the opposite bench. He wondered if she considered the broom to be a weapon if she had to defend herself against a retired detective! She peered at him steadily for a few moments before saying anything, then: "You're not going to tell on me, are you? You're not going to have me arrested?"

Pete shook his head vigorously. "No, I am just a friend of Mrs. Erickson, and I want to be your friend, too. You have nothing to be afraid of."

He heard what might have been a small sigh coming from this thin woman. "Can't they put that man away again? I know he killed her. I know they let him out of prison. I read that." Her tone seemed one of indignation, not fear.

"Maybe if there is some new evidence we can do something more. Will you tell me, like you told Mrs. Erickson, about what you saw the last time you saw Miss Hubbard? When you saw her in the car with somebody else?"

Mrs. Elijah frowned. Pete thought that she must be thinking he was either simple-minded or forgetful or both, for surely she would believe Zora had told him everything from their earlier conversation. "I wasn't spying!" She said indignantly. "I wanted to say 'good-by' to Miss Jane. There was a woman in that car, and Miss Jane got in. That woman was big. Bigger than me. Bigger than Miss Jane. But she was sitting down so I don't know how big. She had on dark glasses. And a hat." There was a pause. Then, in a quieter voice, she continued, "I guess it could have been a man." Pete noticed that she didn't say anything about the undelivered chocolates.

"Did they talk to each other? Could you hear anything?"

"I don't know. I guess they talked. I couldn't hear."

"Were they in the car very long after Miss Jane got in?"

"I don't think so. I think I heard the motor running. Then they left."

"Who drove the car when they left? Do you remember that?"

A frown. "Not Miss Jane. That person in the car. They drove away fast."

"Do you think Miss Jane saw you there? Do you think she was afraid and didn't say anything to you?"

A look of concentration. Finally, "I don't know. She was always nice to me. She always brought me chocolates. But they drove away fast."

"I don't suppose after all this time you would remember the license plate?"

A shake of the head, "no."

"Did you tell anyone at the home about seeing Miss Jane in the car?"

Now he saw a look of alarm on her face and hoped he had not gone too far.

"No! I didn't tell anyone! I wasn't doing anything wrong!"

Pete said nothing for a few moments. Mrs. Elijah was looking down now, and he sensed he would get little, if anything, more from her. He stood up. Reaching for his wallet, he extracted one of his business cards, this one with only his personal information on it, and not his title as a retired detective with the Columbus police. He moved over to her bench and bent down, holding out the card. "Here. I want you to have this. If you remember anything more about that day or about Miss Jane, I would like you to call me. Can you do that?"

She held out the card, looking at it. Suddenly, she looked up at him. "Do you have many grandchildren?" The question caught him by surprise, and he had to think about how to embellish his previous lie. "Three, and they are a handful." He mentally asked his

older daughter to forgive him for embellishing on the one grandson she had produced. She nodded. "I don't have any." He did not know what to say, so he offered his hand. She took it reluctantly but her handshake was surprisingly firm. "I hope you can put him away for good," she said, and he knew she was referring to Parch. How much did she really know? Was all of her story made up? But she hadn't tried to claim the person in the car with Jane was anyone she could recognize – not even the gender.

"Thank you, Mrs. Elijah. You have been a help. I will tell Mrs. Erickson that, too." He started walking toward the parking lot, and then he heard her call after him, in a surprisingly strong voice, "Her car – it was blue." He turned around. The woman was disappearing into the home, and the door closed behind her. Unaccountably, he felt a shiver. Jane Hubbard's car was blue. So at least it was possible the car she was last seen in was her own. But what did that mean? That she knew the driver or that someone had gotten a hold of her car? Or was it even her car? How had they all missed talking to Mrs. Elijah? And how much had he discounted what Zora Erickson might find out?

On his drive back to Columbus, he reviewed his conversation with Mrs. Elijah. Then, he thought about his meeting with Zora. Unbidden, the voice of his late wife, Regina, came to him so clearly he clutched the steering wheel hard. "You should trust her. You should talk to her." In the next few seconds, he visualized Zora and realized that she did in some ways remind him of Regina. And strangely, that thought gave him a feeling of assurance. He decided to be a little more willing to communicate with Zora Erickson.

CHAPTER TWELVE

Zora felt that at least two people on Tyler's list of three might be able to tell her something about Jane and the long ago affair, "but I mustn't get my hopes up", she thought gazing at the names the next morning. She decided to start with Leona de Santos. A phone number in Tucson was listed. It was too early in the morning for a call to that time zone, so Zora spent some time at her computer, continuing to outline the steps she had already taken, what she had learned and her options for what to do next. Then, at noon Boston time, she made the call.

A female voice answered: "Ms. de Santos' residence. May I help you?"

"Good morning. My name is Zora Erickson, and I am trying to get in touch with Mrs. de Santos. She doesn't know me, but I am trying to locate an old friend who may have been a student of her husband at the University of Illinois many years ago. May I ask to whom I am speaking?"

"I'm Sara, her daughter. Mother is resting right now. I can talk with her later and see if she can call you back." There was a pause. "Actually, Mother likes company. Do you live far away? She'd probably enjoy a visit."

Zora laughed. "Yes, I'm afraid I don't live very close to Tucson. I'm in Boston."

"Oh, well. But Mother likes to Skype, so maybe we can do that with you later today? If you give me a number where I can text you, I can let you know if she's up to it – if that's all right."

"That's fine, Sara. And thank you." Zora read out her cell phone number.

"Thanks. I've written that down. I'll tell Mother and text you."

As it turned out, Leona de Santos was delighted to "meet" Zora. So, two hours later, Zora was sitting in front of her screen and introducing herself to an animated little lady with a pleasant smile and a head of white, curly hair who was sitting on a sofa next to a woman with tinted glasses, whom Zora judged to be in her fifties.

"Mrs. de Santos, it's very kind of you to meet with me like this. I think Sara told you why I called?"

"Oh, yes, Mrs. Erickson. And what is the name of the student you want to know about?"

"Her name was Jane Hubbard. She was an education major, but I don't know if she actually took any courses with your husband."

Leona de Santos sat up even straighter on her couch. "Oh, Jane! We knew Jane well. James was one of her teachers, and she used to babysit for us – for Sara. I've often wondered what became of Jane. She was such a beautiful girl, so kind, so good with children. I hope she had a large family herself."

Zora was startled; she had not expected Leona's instant recognition of Jane. "I wish I could tell you that she did. But she never married. We taught together in Ohio many years ago. Jane taught English. She was a very dedicated teacher and her students loved her. I moved away from Ohio a long time ago, and I live in Cambridge, Massachusetts now. Jane stayed in Dublin, Ohio, and retired at 62. Shortly after that she went missing. It's been almost thirteen years, and she has never been found. She is listed as 'presumed dead' by the police." She paused. How to ask the questions she needed to ask? She couldn't very well say, "I'm suspicious of the wife of the professor Jane supposedly had an affair with – would that be you?"

"But that's terrible! Did the police suspect somebody?"

"Yes, a broker who swindled Jane, but they could never prove it. He went to jail for swindling clients, including Jane, but he never confessed to harming her. I know it's been a long time, but I'm retired and a widow myself, and I finally decided someone needed to find out what happened to Jane. To let her story have an ending."

"You are right to do that. So right! James would say that, too, I know. He was very fond of Jane and always thought she would make a good teacher." Leona was nodding as if to reinforce her words. "What is it you want to ask me about Jane? I will try to tell you anything I remember. Do you think something that happened in Illinois, at the university, might be connected to this?"

"I'm not sure." Zora needed to choose her next words carefully. "There was a rumor that Jane was dating someone at the university. He might have been on the faculty, and he might have been married. I have no details, and this is very much third-hand."

"She never told you about it?"

"No, I heard it quite recently from another friend of hers but I have no way of knowing if it's true."

"Did this other friend mention a name of the person Jane might have been seeing?"

"Not a full name. Apparently, one time Jane mentioned something about someone named 'Jamie' but she never talked about him again."

Leona was now frowning. Her daughter looked into the camera with an expression Zora could not read. Leona seemed to be collecting her thoughts.

"If you are wondering if this 'Jamie' was my husband, the answer is 'no'. He would never have had a relationship with a student. We were happily married; we did everything together. He was very critical of other teachers who sometimes dated their female students."

Zora waited.

"I don't remember Jane having a steady boyfriend. She was popular – voted most popular in her class or something like that one year, I think. But she never brought anyone around to meet us, and we were very close to her during her last two years in college. That was when she babysat for Sara. I wish I could help you more, but I don't think I can."

"Thank you, Mrs. de Santos, I . . ."

Leona interrupted her. Sitting up very straight on the sofa, she peered at Zora. "You must have tracked me down from records at the University. Are you looking for other former professors or perhaps students named 'James'?"

"Yes. I have two names of other professors. Perhaps you knew them." Zora read off the other two names Tyler had given her.

"We knew them both. I can't conceive of either of them having a relationship with Jane. We always thought Brad was gay. Of course, many things were probably happening then that we didn't know about. But one other thing: no one ever called my husband 'Jamie'. He always insisted on using his full name, 'James' although once in awhile someone would call him 'Jim'."

"I see. This has been helpful, Mrs. de Santos. If you think of anything more, please call me. I gave Sara my number. Thank you both. I will let you know if I find out anything finally about what happened to Jane."

After they disconnected, Zora got up and walked around her living room for several minutes. Another blind alley. She was beginning to wonder if she was missing some track that would be more productive when her phone rang.

"Hello, this is Zora."

"Mrs. Erickson, it's Sara Calisher – Leona's daughter. Am I disturbing you?"

"No, this is fine." Puzzled, she waited.

"I'm outside Mother's house on my cell phone right now. This may be nothing, but I remembered something about Jane. I was nine and ten when she used to babysit with me. She always treated me like a grown-up and I wanted to be just like her. We talked a lot about books and music, and one time she brought over a book of paintings and explained to me about the artists – they were all early American, if I remember. Then she said something like, 'I'm taking a course in art history and I love these paintings so much.' I think I said I would like to take the course, too, someday. And I remember that she laughed and said, 'well, maybe, but I'm taking it with a visiting professor, and he's only here for a year.' Then later when we were leafing through the book, she said something about 'Jamie said this artist was Navaho.'"

"And you think this visiting professor could have been her 'Jamie'?"

"I don't know. I don't think she ever mentioned him again. The classes he taught would probably have been in Arts and Sciences, not in the College of Education where Dad taught. I didn't want to say anything when we Skyped earlier in case Mother thought I was just passing on gossip or implying something about Jane that wasn't true. We all liked Jane very much. But I did want you to know."

"Sara, this could be helpful. It' a long shot that anything that happened to Jane while she was in college is relevant to her death so many years later, but I'm trying to look at every angle."

"Would you like me to see if I can find out anything more about this professor? Mom and I still have contacts back at the university."

"Thanks, but I have my own source there. If there are any records of another professor maybe in Arts and Sciences with the first name of 'James' I think I can uncover them. As I told your mother, I'll keep you informed."

"I'm so sorry about Jane. That she had to die without anyone knowing where or how. Yes, please, let us know what you find out."

Zora moved swiftly to her computer. The email to Tyler was brief. It read: "Can you, please, ask your friend Emile if the U of I employed a visiting or part-time faculty member with the first or middle name of 'James' in the college of Arts and Sciences at the time Jane was in school there?" She knew he would get back to her, even if it took a few days.

She had one more call to make today: to Carl James Armillato in Boulder, Colorado. According to Tyler's description, Professor Armillato would be about 88 now. Zora decided to Google him first. She found confirmation of the address, a list of a few publications – primarily articles in philosophical and educational journals – and a relative by the name of "Bonnie" listed as "deceased". "Probably his late wife," Zora thought. So, even if she reached him and he would talk, and even if on the extremely remote chance that Mrs. Armillato had a been a jealous wife who somehow had sought out Jane many years later and murdered her, this information was not likely to come out in a phone call! "But I have to cover all the bases," Zora told herself. She waited until 4 p.m. – 2 p.m. Boulder time -- to make the call.

The voice answering the phone sounded weak, but clear. "Hello. This is Carl Armillato."

"Professor Armillato, my name is Zora Erickson. We have not met, but your name was given to me by Dr. Emile Chastain, President of the University of Illinois. I am trying to locate an old friend of mine who has been missing for some time. She was a student – undergraduate and graduate – at the university some fifty-five years ago. She majored in education. Her name was Jane Hubbard."

"Jane? Jane Hubbard? Of course I remember her – she was my teaching assistant for one semester. A beautiful girl. Gifted. I had hoped she would stay on to get her doctorate, but I believe she needed to work. Please tell me what happened to her." His voice sounded stronger now.

Zora recited Jane's story briefly. Now, to ask her questions. "Professor Armillato, did you ever know her to be dating any other students, perhaps another teaching assistant, or even a young professor?"

"So you think someone from way back then may have been involved in her disappearance so many years later? No, I didn't know much about her personal life, but you must have some reason to ask."

Zora thought fast. Here was an intelligent man who seemed willing to cooperate but suppose he was "Jamie"? "Yes, from one person who knew her well years later I have learned that she may have had a married lover."

"And do you have a name?"

"No, but one of his names may have been 'James', however, this is very third-hand information."

Unexpectedly, Carl James Armillato laughed. "Well, I wouldn't have minded dating Jane – if I weren't so much older than she was and not in a wheelchair. Ms. Erickson, I had polio when I was very young. I eventually found a wonderful woman to marry me and share my life. She died a few years ago, and I miss her to this day. But I did not go around campus dating anybody, believe me."

Zora felt both embarrassed and let down. "It is very kind of you to share your personal information, Professor Armillato. Please forgive me for asking."

"I don't mind at all. You are doing something noble in trying to find Jane. I feel terrible that she died and no one knows what happened to her. But I just don't recall anything that could help you, I'm afraid. However, if you will give me your email address, I will let you know if I remember anything. And perhaps you could let me know eventually how your search turns out?"

Zora gave him her address and thanked him. Another dead end, or so it seemed.

At five o'clock when Zora checked her emails, she was surprised to see Pete Le Gall's name appear. When she clicked on the message, it was short: "I have thought about our conversation and went to see Mrs. Elijah. She confirmed what she told you. Please send me any updates on new information you get. It might be useful to talk by phone if you prefer. If you are coming to Columbus, we could meet again."

Zora thought for a few minutes. Was he being patronizing? No, it didn't sound like it. She debated about a response and finally typed, "Appreciate your note. I will stay in touch. If you have any reason to come to Boston, we could also meet here."

CHAPTER THIRTEEN

The next morning, Zora made the trip to Braintree to see her grandchildren. It was her granddaughter's seventh birthday. Roy and Kressida were giving a party. Being around fifteen seven-year olds was stimulating but tiring, and when Zora returned to her town house at ten o'clock that night, she was exhausted.

She did check her email and found a brief note from Tyler, acknowledging hers and saying he would get back to her when he heard from Emile. "Too late to do anything more now," she thought, "but in the morning I need to move on my next steps." She was about to log off her computer when an email popped up. She did not recognize the name but opened it anyway.

"Have you found out anything more about your friend, Jane Hubbard? I would like to hear from you." It was signed "Germaine". Surprised, Zora sent a brief note back: "Thank you for writing. I have not found out anything very useful at this point, but I will be in touch. I hope you are keeping well." She had no idea what triggered Germaine's interest but did not want to drop the contact. "I still feel there is more she could tell me," she admitted to herself, before turning out the light.

The following day, she looked up the contacts Phyllis had given her for Jane's second cousin, Hal Hubbard, who was now living in Princeton, New Jersey. Zora felt sure she had never met him, so she thought an email might be the best approach. In it, she introduced herself, told him briefly about her quest to find out what happened to Jane, and asked him to contact her.

When she returned from running errands several hours later, she was gratified to find an answer from Hal. "By all means, let's talk. I could meet you in New York City or invite you to Princeton? Brian and I would be delighted to see you. Or, I could come even come to Boston. What is your calendar like for next week, say Thursday or Friday? I appreciate what you are doing for Aunt Jane."

"And who is Brian?" she wondered. "Probably a partner or husband." She Googled his home address and decided it would be easy to drive to Princeton from Boston. She emailed him that she could come on Thursday and meet any time that afternoon or evening. He replied promptly, inviting her to stay overnight, and she accepted.

She entered the date on her calendar and then said to herself, "what's next?"

Suddenly she wanted more than anything else to talk to Ellie. She called Ellie's cell phone and found her about to leave the university, where she had been doing some research. Classes were not in session.

Thirty minutes later, Ellie was sitting on Zora's high-walled patio, surrounded by her blooming geraniums. They were drinking tea, accompanied by ginger snaps.

Ellie heard all of Zora's report on what she had learned so far and reflected. "Who else are you planning to talk to? I mean, if none of what you have found out so far leads anywhere?"

"There are still a couple of teachers who taught at the same time we all did in Dublin - I could contact them. And I've thought of trying to question Parch's parole officer, not that he – or she - would necessarily tell me anything."

"I'm sure Tyler will get back to you if he gets any mpre information from Emile. But I guess that may not lead anywhere, either. What about Parch himself? I know you told us earlier that you would save him 'til last. Is he still alive?"

"So far as I know. His ex-wife gave me his address. He's in some kind of assisted living in Virginia. He probably wouldn't see me, though."

"But he might. And if you're careful, what have you go to lose? It's not like you're asking him to confess to something."

Zora raised an eyebrow. "I'm not?"

Ellie felt relieved that Zora's sense of irony was still intact. "Well, you wouldn't approach it that way, I suppose. You would probably just ask him if after all this time he had thought of anyone who might be her enemy. And you could watch his face."

"I doubt very much that he would give anything way, and I don't know if even now he's immune from further prosecution. If he killed her – or had her killed – he hasn't told anyone up until now. So, why me?"

"Because maybe he wants to confess. Maybe he wants to get this out. Maybe he's not well and it's a burden for him. I don't know, but I just have the feeling you should see him."

Zora looked at Ellie questioningly, waiting for her to go on.

"I mean, you're good with people. You have a sense. You always knew when I was up or down or undecided when I lived next door to you. You always asked the right questions."

Zora closed her eyes for a moment to consider. She couldn't argue with anything Ellie said. And, truth to be told, she had been thinking of exactly this for some time now – that it was time to see Parch. She opened her eyes and smiled at Ellie. "Thank you for the compliments. I'm not sure I deserve them, but I think you're right – that I need to interview Parch. Or at least try. I'll see Hal Hubbard, although I don't expect to learn much from him. Gather my thoughts after that, and try to see Parch."

"Do you want me to go with you if you can see him?"

Zora had thought about this before she called Ellie. "I might. Let's see how things go next week and if anything else turns up. I'll call you before I set up anything with Parch."

As she emptied that dishwasher late that night, Zora's arms began to tingle – a sure sign that something was bothering her or that she was trying to resurrect a thought. "Maybe in the morning I'll figure out what I can't put my finger on," she consoled herself.

* * *

Later that night a phone rang in a location far distant from Boston. It was answered with a brief "Hello?"

"Someone is investigating."

"Who?"

" A Zora Erickson."

Silence on the other end. Then, "I see. I'll get back to you." The line went dead. Such a careful plot – and to have it undone now. This could still be dangerous. How to deal with Zora Erickson? Time to make a new plan?

CHAPTER FOURTEEN

Zora turned into Hal Hubbard's willow lined driveway just after two o'clock in the afternoon on the following Thursday. Several days before the trip, she had reconsidered his offer to have her stay with him and had made a reservation at a nearby Marriott. Her excuse to him, in an email, was that she really liked her privacy and that being an insomniac, she might want to leave very early the next morning to return to Cambridge. From the beginning of her search, she knew that Hal himself had to be considered a suspect in Jane's disappearance, even if the police had found no evidence to implicate him. Seeing the sprawling, immaculate white ranch-style home with knock-out roses lining the entrance, she chided herself for her suspicions. "But better to sleep in a strange hotel bed than in the house of a possible killer," she told herself with a wry smile.

A thin, red-headed man with a crutch under his left arm, met her at the door. "You must be Zora!" he said, with a wide smile while reaching out to shake her hand. "I'm Brian." She took his hand and glanced down. "Did you break something?"

"Bone in my foot. Stupid soccer game. Please come in. Hal went down to the Publix to get something for dinner. I'm cooking tonight, but it's awkward for me to shop with this crutch."

The door shut behind her, and Zora looked around. Her first impression took in the eclectic but comfortable looking furniture in an array of bright colors and the book shelves that covered two walls. Just then, a miniature black poodle came bounding out of what appeared to be the dining room. Brian reached down awkwardly, balancing his crutches, and grasped the little dog's collar. "Herbie – don't jump on Ms. Erickson!" The dog promptly sat down and eyed Zora.

"He's usually well behaved but he gets excited when someone comes. I hope you don't mind dogs? I can lock him up in our bedroom."

"Oh, please don't do that. I do like dogs. My husband and I used to have a collie."

"I would love a collie, but Hal's more or less allergic, and poodles don't shed. Would you like some lunch? I hope your drive wasn't too bad."

"Actually, I stopped for a bite an hour ago, and, no, the drive was fine. Thank you." They were both still standing in the living room, and suddenly Brian said, "Where are my manners? Please sit down – all these chairs are really comfortable. I was making tea for myself – would you like some?"

"That would be perfect, thank you, and I don't take anything in it." Zora picked an overstuffed turquoise chair and sat down. "More like sank down," she thought to herself as the large cushion slowly enveloped her.

When Brian returned with a mug for her and then one for himself, Zora decided to use the time before Hal came home to some advantage. "Brian, I don't really know anything about what you and Hal do. Do you work in Princeton?"

"We're both in IT. Hal works for ETS here in Princeton. I work at home but commute about twice a month into the City to the bank. Fortunately, I haven't had to do that since I got this cast on – should be off in two weeks." He poked the crutch disapprovingly at his heavily wrapped right foot. "If I had to move into Manhattan to work, I wouldn't do it. I'd resign first. Hal and I found this house five years ago, and we love it here. We're still decorating the basement, doing a sports theme, adding a bar. It's fun. And you live right in Boston?"

"In Cambridge. I have a townhouse. I like it but sometimes I miss having a bigger house. I gave up a lovely one when my husband died." Zora was about to describe the gallery she and Rashad had run, when she heard footsteps. She looked up to see Hal Hubbard entering from the dining room and, presumably, from the kitchen. With some difficulty, she pulled herself up from the enveloping chair. "Hal, I'm Zora Erickson."

"Zora! So pleased to meet you. And you came all this way – please sit down and be comfortable. I see Brian is being a good host. If you'll excuse me a minute to put away my groceries, I'll be right back."

Zora watched him leave the room. A well-built man, probably in his mid-forties, she assumed. Muscular but not fat. Dark black hair, big hands. "Could this man possibly be a killer?" she asked herself. Her instincts all said "no" but she knew she must be careful about jumping to conclusions.

When Hal had taken a seat across from her and they had exchanged a few pleasantries about her trip, he put down his tea and said, "Now, please, ask me anything you want – I honestly don't know if I can shed any light on Jane's disappearance after so many years, but I'll try and I would be interested in what you have learned."

"Well, I'm not completely clear on how you and Jane are related, so perhaps you could tell me that."

"Of course. Her older brother was my grandfather. Grandfather has been dead for more than twenty years, and my dad – his son and Jane's first cousin – died of cancer in his sixties. I've known Jane all my life although I didn't see her often. I did try to visit her once a year or so after I got out of graduate school and started work. By then, we were a very small family – my dad and grandfather were gone, and aside from me, Jane had just her mother, who died several years before Jane retired, and an old great aunt, who was related on her mother's side. That was it."

"And you were the executor of her will? How did you learn of her disappearance?"

Hal looked past Zora for a moment, staring out the picture window at something she could not see.

"The police called me after a week. Phyllis had reported to them that Jane didn't return that Saturday from visiting her great aunt. They had found her abandoned car and were checking out all possibilities. Phyllis gave them my contacts. I visited Jane about two months before that but had not heard from her since. I was living and working in Dallas at the time, so casual visits were not easy, although we had talked about Brian and me spending Thanksgiving in Columbus with her the following November. After the police called, I got in touch with Phyllis. It wasn't clear what should happen next so I contacted a lawyer in Columbus through a friend of mine. I had a copy of Jane's will, of course, but I didn't know what to do. He urged me to come to Columbus – I had been on an assignment in Cincinnati for two weeks – so I got there quickly."

His gaze turned back to Zora, and she saw what looked like sadness in his eyes. "That must have been very difficult for you. Were you allowed in Jane's apartment when you got there?"

"Yes, the lawyer had gotten permission from the Court, so I was allowed in. The police had searched the apartment, of course, but since Jane was just missing and not declared dead or even the object of foul play, there wasn't much more they could do. The only thing they asked was that the detective on the case come into the apartment with me when I first went in."

"And did you do your own search? You must have known at least some of the things Jane had since you had been there before. Was there anything missing?"

"Not that I could see. I do remember that there was a small cabinet next to her bed drawer at the bottom that could be locked. It wasn't locked, though. The only things in it were some costume jewelry and a small purse full of foreign coins. I don't know if Jane used to keep anything else in there. She had some paintings that she had always told me were originals, but there didn't seem to be anything of significant value. Later, when I had things appraised, the value of everything in the apartment came to under twenty-thousand dollars. I didn't sell or give away anything until Jane was officially declared dead, except for a couple of small items to Phyllis."

"What about her books? I know she had a big library."

Hal waved his hand toward the far wall of the living room. "Yes, and there they are. She had left them all to me. When I was finally allowed to move things out of the apartment, I boxed them up. Until Brian and I moved here, I kept the books in storage. Now, finally we have room for them."

"How long have you and Brian been together?" Zora knew the question might seem impertinent but she was genuinely curious.

For the first time since meeting her, Hal smiled broadly. "Fifteen years." We met through a mutual friend. We got married five years ago, just before we bought this house.

"It's a lovely place, Hal. Do you mind if I ask you some other questions about you and Jane?"

"Please do."

"As her executor, you knew the contents of her will. How much of an estate did she leave?"

"Very little, as it turned out. Her mother hadn't left her much of anything, so there was no inheritance from her. Jane had one insurance policy for twenty-five thousand dollars. I was the beneficiary. Jane always said that would be enough to take care of her funeral expenses and leave a little for me, which I told her I did not need. As things turned out, I spent some of it on the lawyer and the work to probate her will after she was officially declared dead. After that, I was able to sell all the things from her apartment and I gave all of the proceeds from the sale to a non-profit for children's literacy that Jane had named in her will. There was only about $1500 in her checking account. I set up a savings account for that. It's grown a little bit in the twelve years since. I guess I always hoped we would hear from Jane."

"What money do you think she was living on? It doesn't sound like she had much."

"She was looking at applying for Social Security; I found the forms on her computer. And she had the retirement program from the school system, so I suppose she was all right. I never knew how much Parch swindled her out of, but clearly she felt she had enough to retire."

Zora got up and walked over to the bookshelves. She glanced back at Hal. "He didn't get much from her estate," she thought to herself, "so what would be his motive if he did anything with Jane?" There didn't seem to be one. Out loud she asked, "Did you have the books appraised, too?"

"Yes, but there were no first editions or rare copies, so I think they were valued at less than two thousand dollars."

A muffled crash came from the kitchen, followed by a loud "DAMN!"

"Oh, dear, Brian's probably having trouble managing with his crutches. Let me go check. I'll be right back." Hal leaped up and disappeared from the living room.

Zora faced the rows of books, neatly arranged by author. There were the Jane Austen's. A handsomely bound Dickens collection. All of Faulkner, whom Zora confessed to herself she had always had trouble reading. Collected plays of Tennessee Williams, Arthur Miller, and Eugene O'Neill. Some volumes on music, some on art. Nearly half a shelf on geography and travel. She remembered Sara de Santos Calisher's story about the art book featuring Native American painters, but nothing on any of the shelves matched that description. "Maybe it was a library book or a text book she sold later," Zora told herself. Not that finding it would mean anything, unless the mysterious "Jamie" had signed it and she could finally discover his last name. And how likely was it that he was in any way connected with all this anyway?

Hal returned, Herbie at his heels. "Sorry about that. Brian just dropped a pan. Nothing broken. I need to take Herbie for a short walk. Would you like to come with us or rest here? You're certainly welcome to look through Jane's books – or take one if anything appeals to you."

"That's very kind of you. I was wondering if Jane left a listing of all her books, or if you made one?"

"She did leave a list in a desk drawer, although I think she had not kept it up to date, judging from the date on it. I can make you a copy, if you like. It's in my desk, and we have a printer-copier in Brian's office."

"That would be fine. Thank you. And I think I'll stay here and maybe see if I can help Brian in the kitchen. I'm good at peeling potatoes."

Hal laughed. "All right, you can ask him. He could probably use the help. Herbie and I will be back soon."

It turned out that Brian welcomed Zora's help, especially with breaking the stems off the fresh asparagus and washing the new potatoes, while he went through the additional preparations for their dinner. "Salmon aspic and then some beef birds," he explained, hauling out his "Art of French Cooking" from a low shelf. They visited amiably about food, his work, Hal's work and Herbie. Zora asked a discrete question now and then to see if she could ascertain anything about Hal's financial situation twelve years ago or anything else Brian might tell her about what he knew of Jane, but nothing significant emerged.

After Hal returned with Herbie and fed him, they all adjourned to the back yard with gin and tonics. Hal and Brian regaled Zora with stories about Princeton and renovating their house. Hal set the table outside for dinner since it was such a warm evening. Brian's first course, the fish, emerged on white and blue China plates at 6:05 p.m., and Hal brought out chilled Chablis. The beef course followed, with Zora's carefully prepared vegetables and a Malbec, and the meal ended with a strawberry tart. By 9 p.m., Zora was suppressing a yawn.

"This has been a most enjoyable evening, and I thank you both. I should be getting back to my hotel. I want to be back in Cambridge tomorrow as early as possible."

"We were so glad you could come! Let me make you a copy of Jane's index of her books and then get you on your way." Hal excused himself from the table.

With the two pages of paper in hand, Zora thanked her hosts again. "I will stay in touch and let you know if I find out anything about Jane. I have not given up hope."

"And she would appreciate it," Hal said, taking both of Zora's hands in his own large ones. "She spoke of you more than once, and I know she valued your friendship. Thank you for all that you are doing."

Back at the Marriott, Zora unfolded the list of books. It was entitled, "Library of Jane M. Hubbard." All the entries were in Jane's hand-writing. They were not strictly in alphabetical order. "Probably she added titles as she acquired them," Zora thought. She did notice that a few titles had been erased. "Did she give these away? Lose them? Destroy them?" It was difficult to see any of the letters that had been erased. On one line, it looked like the word "art" may have been in the title, but it was not clear. Zora sighed. Perhaps this book would have had an inscription – perhaps from "Jamie". But it was gone now, and she realized that despite a very pleasant day, she was no further along in solving Jane's mystery than she had been twenty-four hours ago.

CHAPTER FIFTEEN

Sitting at her desk the following afternoon, Zora determined to reconsider the things that were bothering her most about Jane's disappearance.

"For example, why didn't Hal find anything more than costume jewelry and a few foreign coins in an unlocked drawer in Jane's bedroom? I don't remember Jane's wearing a lot of jewelry, but certainly she had more than a few cheap pieces. In fact, I think I do recall one really striking turquoise broach."

Was it possible that someone had gotten into Jane's apartment and taken things? Even though neither Phyllis nor Hal had mentioned being aware of anything missing, it was possible they would not know.

And, whatever Parch did or did not do, there was the unexplained lipstick on the tissue in the Jane's car, plus the cigarette ashes. "Were these planted to put the police off the trail and make them think there was a woman involved? Or *was* there a woman involved? And was she working with Parch?"

For that matter, why hadn't Parch fought back harder when the sentencing judge virtually accused him of killing Jane? Did his lawyer advise otherwise, or did Parch have no defense?

Jane had seemed to lead an exemplary life, yet there were at least three candidates in addition to Parch who might have wanted to harm her: Parch's wife, Mai, who could have thought Parch was having an affair with Jane or that Jane would further incriminate Parch in the swindle; Germaine St. George, who might have been in love with Parch despite everything and not wanted Jane to testify against him; and the unknown wife of the mysterious Jamie, if she knew about their affair. Hal was a very outside possibility, "but I don't see that he had any motive," she concluded. For now, she ruled him out.

"Phyllis may be able to answer a couple of questions," she decided and made the call.

"Are you going to tell me what you've found out so far?" Phyllis asked. Zora could hear the eagerness in her voice. She described, briefly, her contacts with Leona de Santos and her daughter, plus her more recent visit the Hal Hubbard. Before Phyllis could ask for any more details, Zora said, "Phyllis, do you know if Jane had any out of town visitors shortly before she went missing, or if she was expecting anyone?"

"Not that I know of. Why?"

"Hal said he found only costume jewelry in a drawer in Jane's bedroom – a drawer that could be locked but wasn't. I've wondered if someone either broke in or possibly was a guest who stole something from Jane. Or even someone who broke in after Jane went missing. Someone who may ultimately have wanted to do her harm. Surely she had more than costume jewelry."

"Well, yes she did, although she was not a great one for wearing more than earrings and a watch or maybe a pin. I do remember that she was going to donate some things to a charity auction for the foundation working on literacy. I suppose that she might have given them some pieces. I really don't know. She was quite frugal, especially after she was swindled. Would it help you to know if anyone stayed with her that I didn't know about? Our building has security. I know our resident manager quite well. If all the records haven't been destroyed, I could ask her to go back over the months before Jane disappeared. But I suppose the police have already done that."

"That would be very helpful, Phyllis, thanks. Just let me know what you find out. I may be traveling again in a week or so, but send me an email if you find out anything."

Zora made a note to ask Pete Le Gall whether the police had talked with building security at Oak Manor. She thought she had seen a sentence in the police records to this effect, but now she wanted to be sure.

Just as she was getting up from her desk, Zora saw a new email. It was from Tyler, and it was short. "Emile says the university has no records that far back on visiting or part-time professors. I'm sorry. Let me know if you need anything else." She typed a brief "thank you" and left to take a walk. Sometimes she found thinking was easier when she was moving around.

When she returned from a pleasant stroll around Cambridge and a stop to admire the scullers on the Charles River, she knew three more things she could do right away. The first was a call to Hal. She waited until 5:30 and hoped he was home. She rang their landline so she could talk with Brian if Hal wasn't there, and it was Brian who answered on the second ring.

"Brian, it's Zora Erickson. If I'm disturbing you, I can call back later but I need a favor."

"Perfect timing. I just sent in twenty spread sheets and I need a break. But Hal is not here – he's attending a conference that's going to run late. Can I have him call you?"

"No, I can leave a message with you. And, by the way, thank you for that marvelous dinner. It was a perfect evening."

"Yes, except I'm afraid we didn't help you find Jane. What's up?"

"I think Jane had a friend at the University of Illinois. He may have been one of her professors for a brief time. He may have taught art history or something like that. I don't have his full name, his first name was probably 'James' or 'Jamie'. I saw that Jane had many books on art. I was going to ask if Hal could look through them and see if any of them have a dedication or inscription or even an 'owned by' label, and what name is written there. This is a long shot, but this person may be able to help us find out what happened to Jane."

"Really? Well, I'd be happy to help with that. I've got some time this evening. You know, I really feel bad about your friend Jane. If it hadn't been for her, we wouldn't have been able to afford this house. I'll send you a text if I find anything – and you can call me if I do so I can tell you more"

"That's perfect, Brian. Many thanks. I'll be here."

She hung up, puzzled. Hadn't Hal told her there was only one insurance policy and he had used it to pay bills? But maybe more was left to him than he let on. Could this have been enough of a motive for Hal to do away with Jane? That seemed highly unlikely. Despite her doubts, Zora remembered that she needed to order a "thank you" gift for Hal and Brian for their hospitality. So she spent half an hour on line looking at kitchen accessories she thought they might like, settling on new "rabbit" wine bottle opener.

Finally, she typed a long email to Pete Le Gall, reporting everything she had found out. She wanted to call him, really, hoping that by now he might sound more interested in what she had to say and would encourage her and tell her she was on the right track. But she resisted. "I'll send him another note in a few days and suggest we talk next week," she assured herself. She didn't want to admit that she remembered how pleasant his voice sounded, even thought their first conversation was far from congenial.

After that, Zora knew she must face the next step, "which is not going to be easy." In a facility in Virginia, Murray Parch was undoubtedly keeping secrets. How best to approach him? She felt sure his ex-wife, Mai, had warned him of the investigation Zora was conducting. So, perhaps he would refuse to see her. "Somehow, I've got to confront him before he has time to concoct a story or simply turn me down."

Without taking the time to construct a fool-proof plan, she sent a quick email to Ellie: "Are you up for a trip to Virginia? I may need a wing man while visiting my next suspect." The answer came back within the hour: "When do we leave?"

CHAPTER SIXTEEN

After a more lengthy discussion with Ellie, Zora decided that the best way to interview Parch would be to take him by surprise. If Mai had told him about Zora and that she was trying to find out about Jane, he would likely refuse to see her if she contacted him in advance. Better to just appear and take her chances on seeing him. "And, of course, if he is innocent of anything to do with Jane's death, he may be willing to talk with me."

So they arranged the trip. She and Ellie would fly to Dulles Airport outside of Washington, DC, rent a car, and drive to Winchester, Virginia, where Parch lived in what was described as a "pleasant retirement community with independent and assisted living facilities." They planned to leave the following Thursday in the morning.

"And, of course, the 'best laid plans . . .' and all of that," Zora said to herself, with resignation, when twenty-four hours before their flight, Ellie called. "Zora, I hate to do this to you, but I'm sick. I haven't been feeling well for several days, and I think it's just flu, but Tyler wants me to see the doctor. I have to go in tomorrow. I'm so sorry. Can we postpone our trip? Will the airline let us change the dates?"

"I'm sure they will, but don't you worry about it. Your getting well is more important. I may just go by myself. You know, we've discussed this. There really is no danger for me to see him."

Ellie sighed. "Zora, I'm letting you down and I hate that, but I really wish you would not go alone."

"What if I take my baseball bat?"

It was a private joke between them, and Ellie gave a little laugh. "He wouldn't have a chance! If you decide to go without me, at least text or call us by tomorrow night. If we don't hear from you, I'm going to call the police in Winchester. I mean it."

"All right. Let me think about this. If I go, I'll stay at the hotel near Dulles where we have a reservation. I will call you by 7 p.m. tomorrow. He's not going to do anything to me, at least not while I'm there. If he's hostile, I'll leave quickly. Then we can worry about what he'll do next!"

Zora was joking but Ellie did not take it that way. "Zora, please be careful! You may about to upend this man's life and his carefully guarded secret. If he's killed once, he could do it again. Really, I wish you'd wait for me to get well so I can go with you."

Zora already knew she was going to take the trip. "I'll call you in the morning and let you know what I'm going to do. You just take care of yourself. Tell Tyler I told him to make you hot milk tonight before you go to bed."

On Thursday, at 10:05 a.m., Zora's flight took off from Logan Airport. A few minutes before, she texted Ellie: "I'm going. Will call you by 7." By 12:30 p.m., she was turning the key in the ignition of her rental car at Dulles. At 1:50 p.m., she was in Winchester, passing a pleasant-looking small park, with benches, a fountain, and flowering shrubs. It was on the outskirts of the retirement complex. At 1:55 p.m. she pulled in to the parking lot of the complex itself. Her first impression was of grey concrete. The connected buildings were low, plain, unassuming. There was grass, a few small trees, not much color. "Almost like a prison," she thought, making her way to the main entry.

At the reception desk, a young man sat with the phone tight against his ear, having a very serious conversation. He acknowledged her but kept on talking. Finally, the call ended, and he straightened up. "Hello. May I help you?"

Zora had given a great deal of thought about what she would say. "Yes, thank you. My name is Ellen Sheppard, and I would like to see Mr. Parch. He does not know me, but I am the friend of one of his former clients."

Rather than saying anything, the young man frowned slightly and consulted his computer screen. When he looked up at Zora again, he was frowning even more. "I'm afraid that's impossible. Mr. Parch was taken to our medical facility two days ago." Then, looking around the lobby, where there was no one else in sight, he leaned over even further and said in a low, conspiratorial voice, "His heart, I think. I was off duty. Do you want to leave a message? We could see he gets it."

Zora thought fast. "Oh, I'm so sorry. I'm only in town for one day, and I especially wanted to see him. Where is your medical facility?"

The young man blinked a couple of times. "Just across the road from where you turned in. But I don't know if he can have visitors. Want me to call?" His tone was getting friendlier.

"Do you have his room number at the hospital?"

"*Medical facility.* It's not really a hospital." He returned to his screen. "Yup. Room 129. Don't know as they'd let you see him, though. Is there anything else I can do for you?"

She thought for a moment. "If I can't see him, I would like to call him later, I mean when he gets back here. Do your clients have private phone lines or may I have your switchboard number?"

"Most of 'em have phones in their rooms." He squinted at his screen again, then scribbled something down on a piece of blue paper. "Here's his number for his room. You need anything else?"

"No, thank you. You've been very kind. I'll drive over to your *medical facility* and if I can't see him, I'll leave a message there. Really, you've been very helpful." She gave him her best smile. He simpered. "That's what we're here for. Have a nice day!"

Once across the road, Zora had to think about her next move. Could he have visitors? How tight was their security? Surely the staff would notice a 75-year old black lady whom they had never seen before walking down their corridor. Then she had an idea.

She turned the car around and drove back to the main building. Same desk, same young man, now on his computer. He looked up, surprised. "You didn't find it?"

"I did, but you know, I thought it would be nice to bring him some flowers. And maybe take some to one or two of your other residents if they are in there. Can you direct me to a florist? This is my first time in Winchester, so I don't know my way around. Do you have any ladies living here who are in your medical facility now, too? They might like a little cheer – I know what it's like to be in the hospital and all alone."

The young man's face changed from surprise back to a look that seemed to say, "Well, I find you a little odd but harmless, so I'll help you." He squared his shoulders as if about to undertake a major task. "If you got GPS in your car, I'll write down the address of the florist down town."

"I do, thanks." He started writing. Then, "There's one gal over there who is really nice and she's been in medical about two weeks. Don't know what's wrong with her. Don't think she has much family. If you visited her, I bet she would really like that." He continued writing. "Here's her name and room number."

Zora thanked him profusely, went out to her car, entered the florist shop's data in her phone and found the store within ten minutes. Purchasing one bouquet of pink carnations, she drove back to the small hospital, parked, and went in the front door. A woman in a blue uniform was on the phone. Zora slowed down but kept walking, saying over her shoulder, "Just going to see Mrs. Pirelli." The receptionist nodded and kept on talking.

Fortunately, Mrs. Pirelli was in room 131. A sign at the beginning of the main corridor showed rooms from 101 to 120 going down the left hallway, with rooms 121 to 140 to the right. Zora walked briskly down the right hallway. When she came to room 131, she noted that the door was open. She peeked in. The covers on the bed were heaped so high that Zora barely saw a person under them. Mrs. Pirelli had a crown of white hair and was gently snoring. Zora looked around the room. A hand sink stood to one side of a closet door. She propped up the bouquet in the sink and tiptoed out of the room. Someone would eventually see the flowers and find a vase for them, she hoped. Next stop, room 129.

The door was closed but there was no sign saying "no admittance". If someone was in the room with him, she had her story down. She was Ellen Sheppard, a friend of a friend of a former client. At some point, however, she knew she would have to tell him why she was really there. She pushed the door open.

A man in a robe sat in a wheelchair with his back turned. He was evidently looking out the window. The room felt stuffy. He turned when he heard her footsteps.

So this was Murray Parch. Thinning grey hair, a haggard face, pale, expressionless. She knew he was 66, but he looked at least ten years older. The robe looked too big for him although it was evident that he was a tall man. He clutched the arms of the wheelchair as if to try to stand but didn't. Instead of a normal greeting, he looked at her with the hint of curiosity dawning in his eyes. "Do I know you?"

Zora stood only a few steps from the door. The tingling sensation began in her arms. She did not move toward him. Instead she returned his gaze. "No. We have not met. My name is Zora Erickson. I was a friend of Jane Hubbard. I am trying to find out what happened to her."

CHAPTER SEVENTEEN

Murray said nothing but gestured toward a comfortable arm chair by the bed, near the window. Zora looked around. Her only escape would be out the door where she came in. In his condition, Murray did not look like he could harm her, but perhaps his illness was a fake? But if it was, why? "Come on, Zora, get a hold of yourself," her inner voice said fiercely. She sat down.

He moved his wheelchair to face her, keeping several feet between them.

"You found me through Mai?" He was now looking at her with open curiosity.

"Yes, I visited her. She gave me your address."

"You could have let me know you were coming."

Zora paused. She did not want to let him have the upper hand in this conversation. "Yes, but I didn't – because I thought you might not see me." She paused again. "Mr. Parch, I taught school with Jane many years ago. We were friends. I am seventy-five years old, the same as Jane would be. She had friends, some family, but no one has found any evidence of her in the twelve years since she went missing. I have been feeling guilty for some time that no one, including me, apparently cares enough to find out what happened to her. So I am talking with everyone who might know something. Obviously, you are on that list."

He looked over past her, toward the door. "And I suppose you found Germaine, too. Or maybe all my former clients?"

"I have met with Germaine St. George, yes. She was helpful. She has been the only other client."

"And did she tell you I had an affair with her?"

Zora controlled her expression. "No, but I thought as much."

They looked at each other for a few moments without speaking. Finally, he said, "Fine. Ask me whatever you want. You know, I'm sure, that I've served time and the judge – the *Honorable* Clayton Wyard – gave me extra years because he thought I was responsible for Jane's death. If she hadn't died, I would have spent far less time in prison. But I'm a free man now. Not well, but free. I have a heart condition. Occasionally it acts up. My wife divorced me. I lost my investment business, although a few old friends have been loyal and asked me to consult for them when I got out of prison. I get by at this god-forsaken place. I have nothing to hide. So, what do you want to know?"

Zora took a deep breath. "Was Jane in love with you?"

"No." He stopped, seeming to be thinking of what more to say. Then, "We did not have that kind of relationship although I know some people thought we did. I got her to trust me, we liked each other, and I took advantage of her. She came to our house on occasion; Mai liked her. I slept with other women besides Mai, but at least I didn't take advantage of Jane that way."

"But you did with Germaine?"

"Yes. It was more than a fly-by-night relationship, but then I dropped her. And even though she refused to press charges, I'm sure she hates me to this day."

Zora saw no reason to pursue any discussion about Germaine St. George. Instead, she said, "I would like to know who you think might have killed Jane. You knew her well, I assume. And you offered no defense to the Judge's remarks when he sentenced you. I have wondered about that."

"I don't know who killed Jane. I thought a lot about that before my trial and after it, all those years in prison. I still think about it occasionally, but not as much. I knew I didn't kill her but I had no real defense, although they had no concrete evidence against me. By the time I went to trial, I felt my life was ruined; I was depressed. I guess I didn't really care how many years the judge gave me. I just wanted it to be over."

"And your lawyer didn't tell you to try to defend yourself?

"How could I? I had swindled Jane; they had proof. And I had swindled others. If the judge and maybe others wanted to believe I had done something more, I wasn't in a very good position to defend myself."

They looked at each other for a moment. "What about Julia Lefkowitz? I know you swindled her. Was she in love with you?"

Murray closed his eyes and winced slightly. Zora couldn't tell if it was from a sudden heart spasm or the memories that were coming back to him.

"She trusted me with all her money. I lost most of it. I think she did have a fantasy that I would leave my wife and marry her. She told me that once. I had to tell her that she was wrong. Shortly after that, she killed herself. I realized that she was probably unstable emotionally. I usually went after older women who had seen more of life. Julia was young and vulnerable. I regret that it ended that way."

Zora felt some surprise that he was being as candid as he was – or could it be an act? After all, he had had years to perfect his story.

"But I would still like to know if there is anyone you can possibly think of who might have wanted to do away with Jane? Anything she shared with you? Anything you knew about her?"

Murray shook his head slowly but kept eye contact with Zora. "No, no one. She could be fierce at times, but I only saw that when she was talking about something she was passionate about. Like her students. Maybe she made somebody mad along the way, maybe somebody who carried a grudge – a former student? Another teacher? I didn't know then and I don't know now."

Zora decided to try a different tack. "Where were you on that Saturday, the day Jane disappeared? I've read the court record. You told Mai that you were shopping, but there was no evidence to support that."

"I was with a client. Yes, a woman. A wealthy woman. And, yes, I seduced her to gain her confidence. I did not want to drag her into the investigation, so I never gave out her name. I can tell you who it was, but she's dead now, so she can't tell you anything either."

"Why did you need their money? Were you in financial trouble?"

Murray gave her a tight smile. "You might say that. I was gambling on the side. And I liked expensive cars, expensive clothes, and jewelry -- some of it for Mai, some of it I actually gave to my female clients. Mai didn't know how much we were in debt until the indictment."

Of all the questions Zora had thought she might ask when she confronted Murray, most of them now seemed useless. He was proclaiming his innocence, at least about Jane's death, and he was either an excellent actor or he did not know anything more that could help her. But Zora had one last thread that she wanted to pursue.

"When Jane was investing with you, were you aware of any relatives or close friends that she was planning to leave her money to?"

Murray appeared to be considering the question. "There was her mother, but then she died. I remember that Jane had a second cousin and an aunt who later died, I think. When she set up her account with me, in the paperwork that was required, she designated that in the event of her death, everything was to go to the second cousin, apart from one or two small bequests. Is he still alive?"

"Very much so. But he has not been able to tell me anything useful." Zora did not propose to share any information with Murray, unless it could be used to draw him out. "So she never mentioned a partner or former husband or anyone like that?"

Again Murray appeared to be thinking. "No. She obviously had friends. She liked to travel. She was active in an organization that worked on children's literacy. They were going to get part of her account when she died. Of course, I had taken most of her money."

"Do you know if she had any other money that she hadn't invested with you? I mean apart from her salary and her eventual pension."

"Jane was very cautious. I would be surprised if she hadn't put aside some funds besides what she invested with me. But that never came out when they tried me. And she was supposed to disclose all her financial resources when she opened her account with me, but people seldom really do that. They often have some money on the side. I guess they don't trust their brokers." A hint of a bitter smile passed over his face.

He began to cough and reached for a glass of water near his bed. After he sipped at it, he looked up. His face appeared almost gray. "This is what happens to me now, you see. My heart is betraying me."

Zora stood up.

"I appreciate your talking with me," she said in a level tone. She did not feel anger toward him, exactly, and she still suspected that he knew more than he was telling her. But she did feel some sadness that this evidently sick man could not do much to help her – or himself – at this point.

Murray moved his wheelchair across the room and opened the door for her. "What are you going to do next?" he asked, as she walked around the bed.

"There doesn't seem to be much I can do. I have a few more people to talk to. If nothing comes of that, I will have to admit that Jane's remains cannot be found. There was never a memorial service for her, though, and I would like to arrange that with a few of her friends in Columbus." Then she stopped. She was standing very close to him now. She looked down at him. He seemed to have regained some of his color.

"Did you and Jane ever talk about art?"

He looked puzzled. "Well, yes, we did. Mai was very interested in Southwestern painters and potters. She had a collection. Once when Jane came to dinner, she brought a book about Native American art and loaned it to Mai. Why do you ask?"

"Just another avenue I need to pursue. Not one likely to get me anywhere." She paused. What else was there to say? She looked at him with a level gaze for a minute. "Good-by, Mr. Parch."

He did not respond, and she could not see the look in his eyes as he watched her disappearing down the hallway, away from his room.

Zora got into her rental car and started back to her hotel near Dulles Airport. An idea was forming in her mind. At 7 p.m., she would check in with Ellie. And then she planned to call Mai Parch about a book. Maybe the day had not been wasted after all?

CHAPTER EIGHTEEN

Ellie and Tyler Sheppard both got on the line when Zora called. They listened intently to her description of her meeting with Murray Parch. "I'm just glad you got out safely!" Ellie exclaimed, as Tyler added an emphatic "yes!"

"And how are you feeling, Ellie? I've been worried about you all day."

There was a pause, and Zora drew in a sharp breath. If anything were to happen to Ellie . . . .

"Actually, I'm feeling fine – for someone who is going to have a baby in seven and a half months!"

"Oh, Ellie! That's wonderful. Congratulations to both of you. Did you just find out today?"

"Yes. I've been feeling odd for a couple of weeks. Tyler has been trying to get me to go to the doctor, and I wouldn't."

Tyler interrupted. "But everything is fine, and the doctor told her the morning sickness would NOT last for nine months." Zora heard laughter.

"Well, it doesn't – and I've got a recipe for a tea they make in Botswana that's supposed to cure all kinds of problems. I'll make some for you when I get home."

They discussed getting together soon. When the call was over, Zora felt exhilarated. She took a few minutes to order dinner from room service and then pulled a card case out of her purse. In it was the business card Mai Parch had given her. Zora dialed Mai's number.

After two rings, she heard the voice mail message: "This is Mai. Please leave your name and number." Zora began to leave her name and number when she heard a click and Mai herself came on the line. She immediately apologized for the voice mail. "I did not recognize your phone number. I'm sorry. What can I do for you? Have you found out anything about Jane Hubbard?"

"Mrs. Parch, I saw Murray today. I had been planning to talk with him. Unfortunately, he could not tell me anything that I did not already know. But he did mention one thing and that is why I am calling you."

"Yes?"

"He told me that you and he and Jane had conversations about art, that you like Southwestern art and that maybe Jane loaned you a book about Native American painters. I am very interested in that book. Do you remember it?"

"Yes, but I mailed it back to her a long time ago – before Murray was convicted. Before she disappeared. I could try to find the title; I may have written it down."

"No, I don't really need that – but I'm wondering if you remember anything about the book she loaned you. Did it have any kind of inscription or dedication? I have reason to believe someone gave her that book, and that person may somehow be connected with what happened to Jane."

"I don't think it did. I have a good memory, and I don't recall seeing anything in the book. I do remember that she said it was a favorite of hers. That she would like me to return it eventually because it was given to her by one of her favorite professors. I think she said he was a Mr. James or Jamieson or something like that."

Zora's heart stopped. "Mr. James or Jamieson." Not a first name of "James" or "Jamie" but a *last* name. She forced herself to speak calmly. "And did Jane say more about this professor?"

"Not that I remember. I guess she took a course with him in college or graduate school. That night we discussed several Southwestern artists, and I showed her some of my collection. I've had to sell a lot of it since I've needed the money, but I still have some treasured pieces." Zora could hear the wistfulness in Mai's voice.

"Mrs. Parch, thank you for this. It may be helpful."

"May I ask how?"

Zora hesitated. After all, the Parches were themselves still under suspicion – at least from her. "I'm looking into everything from Jane Hubbard's past. Even old friendships. This may have been one of them."

Mai remained silent for a few seconds. Then, "I see. Please let me know what happens." The line went dead.

And what had Murray told Mai about Zora's visit, if anything? Were they really in touch? Did they work together to kill Jane? "I must not let down my guard against any of these people," Zora told herself. It was late. She wanted to get a good night's sleep before her early morning flight back to Boston. Once there, she would try to find "Mr. James or Jamieson", but was this the wrong track altogether? She could hear Roy's voice telling her early on in her investigation, "The simplest answer is often the right one". "Nothing simple about this case!" she thought, falling into a troubled sleep.

CHAPTER NINETEEN

The letter arrived in the mail three days after the day Zora got home from her trip to Virginia. The time had been gone by quickly while she caught up on emails, paid bills, spent a morning at the beauty salon and checked in with Roy, Ellie and two other friends. For once, the mail was early. She thought it might be a solicitation, since it came in a rectangular, white envelope, with her name and address typed – but no return address. Inside was a white card with a single word on it, obviously cut out of a newspaper or magazine and pasted on the card. In capital letters, it read "STOP". She put it down and felt her chest tighten.

The post mark was legible – New York City and a zip code. The date stamp was blurred; she couldn't read it. She turned the envelope over gingerly. It had a flag stamp on it. Nothing else to see. Her address appeared to have been typed on a computer. Maybe this was, after all, the beginning of some clever marketing campaign, and she would get a follow-on mailing the next day? "Not likely," she thought. She sat for a few minutes to compose herself. "After all, whoever it is isn't threatening to kill me – or to do anything really," she said out loud. After a few more minutes she picked up the phone to call Roy.

"Don't touch it again, Mother!" he said in what sounded like a harsh tone, but she knew he was worried. "I'll be there in an hour." She did not resist.

When he came, he used gloves to examine the envelope and the card inside. He wrote down the Manhattan zip code that appeared over the stamp. He photographed the envelope and the note. "I'll take this to headquarters this afternoon. Have you had any strange calls, or messages, or hang-ups or anything?" They were sitting in her living room, Roy with a cup of coffee, Zora sipping plan seltzer water. It tasted refreshing, and she realized her mouth had been dry ever since she opened the envelope.

"No, nothing like that, Roy. I've been fine. I'm not even sure this is related to Jane."

He looked at her steadily. "You did the right thing to call me. But, mother, maybe it's time to give this investigation a rest? At least for a few days. Have you found out anything at all that you think is significant? Maybe something we could check out? Was there any-one you saw who lives in or near New York City?"

She knew that behind the words, her only son was expressing real concern, and she wanted to make him feel better. She chose her words very carefully. "I don't think I've found out anything that would really lead to Jane's killer." She paused. "I did visit her second cousin and his partner recently. They live in Princeton, New Jersey. Hal – the second cousin – works in Princeton, and his part-ner, Brian, works in Manhattan. But he said he wasn't going into the City just now because of a broken foot. He's on crutches."

"Do you suspect either of them?"

"Not really. They seemed pleasant, straightforward. Brian did mention that they could not have bought the house they own now if it hadn't been for the inheritance from Jane. But Hal seemed to imply that what money she left them was insignificant."

"Who was the last person you saw or talked to about Jane?"

"Murray Parch. He's in an assisted living facility in Virginia, al-though right now he's in their infirmary. I saw him there last week."

"I wish you had told me you were going to see him. I would have advised against it. After all, even his sentencing judge said he thought Parch either killed Jane or contributed to her death."

"And that's why I didn't tell you," Zora said to herself but merely patted Roy's hand.

"Roy, if I had thought I would be in any danger, I wouldn't have gone to see him. He's old and sick and quite possibly dying. I didn't exactly fall in love with him, and I don't think he is someone I would ever like, but he didn't raise my suspicions."

Roy sat back in his chair and drained his coffee cup. "Will you at least give me a few days to investigate this letter? We can try to get prints, maybe some DNA although the stamp looks like it was a stick-on. We probably won't learn much, but I'd like you to stay in touch and let me know if anything else strange happens. And not go out of town. Will you do that, please, Mother?"

Zora nodded and felt a lump in her throat. For the first time since she started trying to find the answer to Jane's disappearance, she wondered if she was doing the right thing. Had she really alerted someone who would now try to harm her? Telling her to "stop" was one thing. But if she didn't, was she in danger? She needed time to sort out her thoughts about this, and she did not want to think out loud with Roy because, she suspected, he would worry even more.

"I'll stay in touch, and I won't go anywhere except to see friends. I'll be fine." She paused. "But I may invite someone here – Detective Le Gall. I've been keeping him informed. After we met in Columbus and then exchanged messages, he said he could meet me again in Columbus, but I think he just might come here. Would you like to see him again? Assuming he can come?"

Roy sat back. Obviously, his mother was full of surprises! "If that's what works for you, I think that's just fine. Let me know the schedule." Secretly, he felt relief that someone other than he, himself, might be willing to keep an eye on her – and maybe even talk some sense into her about this investigation. He rose quickly and gave her a firm hug. "I'll give you a call tonight just to check in. Please keep your cell phone handy. I'll worry if I can't reach you!"

She watched him run down her front stairs and get into his unmarked car. Then, she sat down and booted up her lap top. She composed a quick email to Pete: "Can you give me a call? I have some new information." After sending it, she began to write down the questions she now had and the possible answers.

"First," she typed, "who besides Hal and Brian live close enough to New York City to mail a letter from there? Or, assuming it wasn't mailed directly from there, who might have a friend there to whom the letter could have been sent in order to be forwarded to me?"

"Second, could Murray Parch have had enough time to make up the mailing and send it to someone in New York to send on to me?" Not likely. Her visit to him had been only last week. With a Sunday in between, during which the mail would not have moved. Unless he has an accomplice in New York who put it together for him. She could not rule this out.

Going over the list of people she had talked to so far, the simple answer was that possibly everyone she interviewed would have an acquaintance in New York. But if the letter took that two-step path, when was it originally composed and mailed? The whole process might easily have taken a week, or more, given how erratic the delivery of "snail mail" could be.

"Let's assume it was put together over a week ago. Who did I see or talk to right around that time?" Looking back at her notes, the answer was simple: Leona de Santos and her daughter, Sara, and later, Carl Armillato. None of them seemed likely to be suspects in Jane's death. So, what motive would any of them have to warn her off her search?

And then she remembered – she had also called Mai Parch on the evening of the day she saw Murray. Could the letter have come from Mai? But if it did, how did it reach her so quickly? She typed in Mai's name with a question mark.

The next most possible person she felt could be considered as the author of the letter was Germaine St. George. But, again, the timing seemed odd. If Germaine had any part in Jane's death, then wouldn't she, Germaine, have tried to warn Zora away some weeks ago? Still, she needed to consider both motive and timing for Germaine.

Finally, Zora typed in "Mrs. Jamieson?" Did this person still exist? Was she, possibly, the jealous wife of a long-ago professor who had an affair with Jane? Zora felt, again, the frustration of not being able to get reliable information either about the man or the relationship. She added to her notes: "Need to learn more."

She paused. Easy to do a Google search, at least. Without a first name, she didn't have much to go on but she could at least find out how many people with the surname "James", "Jamison" or "Jamieson" would turn up. She went to a site she had used before and was amazed: Over three thousand surnames of "James" showed up, and "Jamison" accounted for over 120. If she spelled it as "Jamieson", there were over 800.

"This isn't going to work," Zora said to herself. How else could she find the elusive "Jamie"? "Maybe a call back to Leona de Santos?" But then she had a better idea. "I could try Carl Armillato again. He seemed genuinely concerned and willing to help. Even though he taught in the College of Education, he might know someone who could remember "Jamie" from Arts and Sciences.

She scrolled down her list of contacts on her computer. His number came up, and she dialed.

"This is Carl Armillato." She heard his pleasant, rather wispy voice.

"Professor Armillato, this is Zora Erickson again. I am really sorry to bother you, but I have another question if you have a minute. This is about Jane Hubbard."

"Yes, I remember that we spoke. How can I help you?"

"When we talked last time, I was looking for a person who taught at the university with the first name of James. But now it now looks like there was a person with the last name of James or Jamieson, who taught art history during Jane's time in graduate school. And he was probably there for just a year or two. He may have been a visiting professor – I really don't have any details. I do have a good contact at the university, but they have no records that far back for part-time or visiting faculty. So, I'm wondering if perhaps you would know someone who taught in the College of Arts and Sciences who might possibly remember if there was such a person on the faculty."

Surprisingly, Carl Armillato chuckled faintly. "You mean, do I have any *living* friend or friends who might remember your Mr. James? I'm afraid at my age, too many of my old friends and colleagues have left us."

Zora felt embarrassed. Of course, his circle of friends, especially those he taught with, would be getting limited these days.

"Mrs. Erickson, let me think about that. I did know faculty in other colleges, and there is even an informal g-mail network of old professors so that we can stay in touch. I can put out a note on the network and also try to think about anyone I know personally who might be able to help with your mystery."

"That would be wonderful. I hope it's not too much trouble. Thank you."

"I'll call or email you as soon as I have something for you. And I'll begin working on this right now. It will be fun to do a little research, and maybe we'll find out something!" His voice had gotten stronger as they talked, and Zora felt her own spirits rise, even if just a little.

They rose even further when an email popped up on her screen with Pete's address as sender. "How about a call in thirty minutes?" She typed "Fine." Collecting her notes, she decided not to tell him about the threatening letter. But she would tell him everything else she was discovering – even the questions that were bothering her. "At worst, I guess he can dismiss all this as just being irrelevant."

But he didn't. When the call came, they talked for almost an hour. Pete seemed primarily interested in her views on Mai and Hal. And he wanted her to repeat much of what she told him previously about Germaine St. George. He seemed less interested in how Parch appeared to her. "But he obviously is keeping many of his thoughts about this to himself," she reflected toward the end of their conversation. Finally, he asked if she was coming back to Columbus. She hesitated and then confessed that she had received the strange letter. "Roy does not want me to travel just now, which is silly, but I promised him I would stay close to home for just a short time."

There was silence on the other end of the line. "You may be in real danger. I'm going to contact Roy and ask him to send me a copy of the letter and everything he finds out. I think you and I should talk more. You may have uncovered something you don't even realize. If I come to Boston, would that be inconvenient for you?"

Zora felt a real tingle of surprise. "It certainly wouldn't be inconvenient. And I know Roy would be pleased to see you. Can you give me some dates when you could come?"

"I'll email you in the morning. I'm volunteering with a YMCA children's tennis tournament, but that's just a couple of days. I'll let you know."

After the call ended, Zora texted Roy. "Looks like Pete Le Gall is going to visit us. We just talked. I'll let you know his schedule tomorrow." She smiled to herself. "Maybe Roy will think I'm beginning a new friendship, not just playing detective." Well, was she? She acknowledged the possibility.

CHAPTER TWENTY

Three messages were waiting for her in her email the next morning. The first was from Velma Dowd, the manager at German Chocolate and Bakery in Columbus, Ohio. "After we met, I was able to locate our sales records for the month your friend Jane Hubbard might have eaten here or purchased chocolates. There was a credit card receipt with the name "J. Hubbard" on it from the date you were asking about, and the time was 10:05 a.m. It was for a box of assorted chocolates and two chocolate bars. Hope this might be of some help. Please let me know how you make out with your search."

Zora thought for a moment. Did this information prove anything, except that Jane had been alive on the morning she was last seen? And if she had been suspecting that anyone was threatening her, would she have followed her usual routine and bought chocolates on her way to the nursing home? Mrs. Elijah said that Jane did not give her chocolates that day. But perhaps she didn't remember? Or, perhaps the person waiting for Jane in the car had shocked Jane into forgetting about Mrs. Elijah?

The second message was from Pete. "Can get in to Boston by noon a week from next Monday. Staying two nights at the Holiday Inn on Boylston and flying out Wednesday afternoon. Hope this works for you. Let me know." She sent him a quick text, suggesting a lunch meeting when he arrived and also that she would call him to later.

The third email was from Carl Armillato. "I've put an inquiry out on our 'old professors' network about the person you are looking for, and I'm going to make some calls today. I will let you know as soon as I hear anything. Best regards."

She texted Roy about Pete's visit dates and asked Roy when he would like to meet Pete. She acknowledged both of the other emails with thanks and then left the house to do her grocery shopping and a few errands. The day was hot, and she came home feeling tired. Maybe she was getting too old for all this running around? "Not a chance – don't even think that way," she told herself sternly and made a cup of tea to boost her energy.

Just she sat down to enjoy her tea on the patio, her cell phone rang. She recognized Carl Armillato's number. "Mrs. Erickson, this is Carl Armillato. I may have something for you. Early this morning, I had an email message and followed it up with a phone call. It was from a sociology professor friend of mine who taught at the University of Illinois about the same time as I did. He was there for over thirty years. He saw my note on the network, asking if anyone remembered a professor, probably of art history, who had a surname of 'James' or 'Jamieson'. My friend emailed that he might have some information. When I talked with him, he said that he did recall a young visiting lecturer who taught courses in the art department. The reason he remembered was that he attended a couple of this young man's lectures on modern art. He wasn't absolutely sure of the name, but he will check with another colleague who was also on the faculty and will likely know. He thinks the first name was Paul and the last name was James. I'm waiting to hear back, but it might awhile. I just wanted you to know that we could have some progress here."

"Professor Armillato, I'm very grateful. I'll forward to hearing from you. This could be very helpful." Zora put the phone down. Did she really think that information about a long-ago romance that might not even have happened would lead to finding out who killed Jane? It was more than a long-shot, but now she had to follow up every lead, however unpromising it might seem.

She couldn't shake the feeling that she was overlooking something, some piece of evidence that was staring at her, so she began again to review the notes of her visits when her cell phone rang. She did not recognize the number and thought it best to let the phone take a message – if there was one. After the ringing stopped, the message "missed call" came up and also the "message" sign. She clicked on it.

She heard an unfamiliar voice. "Mrs. Erickson, this is Christine Kelly at Carter-by-the-Lake. I'm the assistant manager. I'm calling to tell you that Germaine St. George, who I believe is a friend of yours, has asked me to contact you. She was taken to the hospital this morning with what we believe might be a heart attack. Before she left our residence, she specifically asked that we call you. The hospital is not letting her receive calls or visitors yet, but I wanted to get in touch with you as she asked. You can call me any time. Here is my cell phone number." The message ended with an area code 303 number.

Zora sat back and closed her eyes. What did this mean? Why, of all people, would Germaine have wanted Zora to be notified? Was this going to be some kind of death-bed confession?

She thought back, hard, about her visit to Carter-by-the-Lake. Germaine's recital of her relationship with Parch. The picture on Germaine's bed stand that was turned so Zora could not see it. And then she remembered the phrase that had been elusive in her memory. "He would come to see me – buy me cigarettes . . . ." Cigarette ashes had been found in Jane's car. Jane did not smoke. Neither did Phyllis, who might have ridden with Jane now and then. But Germaine smoked. "White lady – big hands." That was how Mrs. Elijah had described the person who was in Jane's car with her that Saturday at the nursing home. Was that Germaine?

The possible chain of events formed quickly – and sickeningly – in Zora's mind. The still loyal and loving ex-client of Murray Parch was ready to help him, ready to help him do away with the one person whose evidence against him might imprison him for a long time. Maybe he had promised Germaine he would divorce Mai even if he had to go to prison? Maybe that didn't even matter, so long as she could help him? Had she come to Columbus to help him kill Jane and do away with the body or just done it on her own? If any version of this was true, Germaine might now feel remorse and want to tell someone. Maybe after all these years she was tired of carrying a burden of guilt.

Zora picked up the phone and dialed the number Christine Kelly had left for her.

CHAPTER TWENTY-ONE

"Mrs. Erickson? I'm so glad you called. You heard my message?" Zora thought she detected a slight Irish lilt in the soft voice.

"Yes, but tell me, please, exactly what happened to Mrs. St. George."

"I was in my office early this morning – at six a.m. I usually come in early on the days I'm acting manager. Germaine rang her emergency bell just after six, and we sent the on-duty nurse's aide up to her room. She could talk but was complaining of pains in her chest and left arm. I got there just as the aide was convincing Germaine that we had to call an ambulance. At first, she didn't want that, but then she said, 'I suppose I have to go'. Then she asked me to bring her a few things from her closet, and when I came back, she was holding a small, red book. She had torn out a page – it had your name, email address and phone numbers on it. She said, 'This is a friend who needs to know about me. Please call her.' That was it. She seemed to be in more pain after that, but she was never unconscious. The ambulance came in twenty minutes. They took her to Mt. Sinai. I called a few minutes ago and all they would tell me was that she is 'stable'. I know she had a stroke some years ago, but this didn't seem like a stroke to me or the aide."

"She has a niece or nephew, I think, maybe both. She didn't ask you to notify them?"

"No, only you. Her niece lives in Brooklyn and the nephew in Chicago. We will be getting in touch with them. I didn't know if you were a relative. Do you mind my asking – are you?"

Zora took a deep breath. "I'm not, but I think Germaine must have considered me a friend. Perhaps a closer friend than I realized. Could you give me, please, the phone number for Mt. Sinai? I will try to call her later if they will allow me to talk to her."

Christine read out the number, giving Zora time to think about how she would ask the next question - maybe the most crucial one.

"Ms. Kelly, Germaine has some precious things there in her apartment – precious to her at least. Did she take anything besides clothes with her to the hospital?"

"I packed just a few things she asked for. And her purse. And the glasses that were by her bed."

"Nothing else? What about the little red book?"

"No. Nothing else. I think she put the little book in her purse. But it seems like I saw a larger book or picture or something by her bed when I first came in and the aide was attending to her. Now that I think of it, when I came back from the closet, the book or whatever it was there was gone. Maybe she put it in the drawer in her bed stand. I don't know. We were very concerned about her. Does it matter?"

"Of course you were concerned, and Germaine was lucky to have you there. I'm sure her things are being safely looked after."

"Oh, yes. We take good care of our residents, and when something like this happens, we secure everything until we know what is going to happen to them. To the residents, that is. When they are going to come back."

Zora could sense that she had flustered the obviously sincere Christine Kelly. "Thank you, Ms. Kelly, I'm sure you do everything possible. I'm going to call the hospital in a little while, but if you hear anything about Mrs. St. George, I would appreciate it if you would call or text me. It's important that I know what's going on."

"Oh, yes, I will be in touch."

And now what? Get on a plane and visit the possibly dying Germaine St. George to extract a confession? Call Pete and tell him her suspicions and suggest he formally reopen his cold case once again? Roy and maybe even Pete would undoubtedly tell her to "bow out," but she wasn't going to.

Zora reached for her tea and found it cold. She went into the house to make a fresh pot. Just as the water started to boil, her cell phone buzzed insistently. This time, she recognized the number: it was Carl Armillato's. She turned off the stove and answered the phone.

"Mrs. Erickson, I think we've hit the jackpot! My former colleague talked with one other professor friend, and I've received a separate email from another person who taught at Illinois around the same time. They all concur: the young man you and I have been discussing must have been Paul James. He was only at the university for two years, probably as an adjunct or visiting professor in art history. Unfortunately, none of my sources have any idea where he went when he moved on or where he might be now. But perhaps with this information you can find him?"

Zora heard the hopeful tone in Carl's voice. "He really wants to help," she thought, and said warmly, "Yes, you've been wonderful to track this down! I think with a little help from Google I may be able to locate Mr. James." No point in telling him her investigation had just taken a dramatic turn that might lead to the real killer. "I will let you know how this all works out," she promised.

"Thank you! I don't like to think of Jane's death going unresolved. If I've helped you a little to find her, I'm grateful."

Zora went back to her kitchen. With all that was happening, she decided tea time had passed. She opened a cupboard. The fifth of Beefeater that someone had given Rashad the year before he died was still at the back. A small bottle of dry Vermouth sat next to it. She kept olives in the refrigerator. For the first time in many years, Zora craved a martini. Mixing it brought back pleasant memories of having a drink after work with Rashad in their gallery. They would sometimes close for the day and then admire all the beautiful things they had collected and were selling. Occasionally, they spent the time planning a trip for more acquisitions. "And we talked," she said to herself. In some ways, this was what she missed most now – that intimate time of day when sharing with the person you loved was all you needed or wanted. After she stirred her drink, gently, she stared at it. And then she knew what she wanted to do next – she would call Pete.

CHAPTER TWENTY-TWO

"Zora!" She heard his voice, deep and strong, and despite herself, tears came to her eyes and she felt unable to speak – but only for a moment. One sip of her ice-cold martini and she felt better.

"Is this a good time, Pete?" she asked.

"Yes. Just came in from my garage. Been hanging a couple of shelves. Do you have something new?"

She started with the phone call about Germaine and then re-layed the information Carl Armillato had unearthed.

When she finished, he asked, "Are you saying that you have a theory now? That Germaine was involved with Parch and they did this together?"

"Yes, something like that. I suppose Germaine could have been acting on her own -- out of jealousy or to protect Parch. Or maybe he asked her to help him get rid of Jane. But the problem is, we still don't have any hard evidence."

"Are you thinking of trying to talk with her?"

This was exactly what Zora had been thinking for the last two hours. But how to do it without a visit to Denver? And even Pete might not approve of that - Roy certainly wouldn't. So she said simply, "Yes, I've thought about it. What do you think?"

There was a pause at the other end of the line. Then, "Not a good idea, Zora. But your theory may be correct - we wondered if this wasn't maybe a crime with two people involved. Unfortunate-ly, we didn't interview Germaine St. George during the investiga-tion. We didn't have any reason to. I suppose that if we had met with her and had even taken fingerprints, we could have matched them with what we found in Jane's car. But at that time, we didn't consider that angle."

Suddenly, Zora's heart began to pound. "What if you had her fin-gerprints? Could they still be matched?"

"Well, yes, we still have the prints we took from the car in the case file. You will recall from looking at the file that we found Jane's prints, and some from Phyllis McDonald, plus two sets we could never identify – neither of which were from Parch or his wife. I could request to have the case put back on active status and try to get prints from Germaine now. That might be difficult without something more specific to tie her to Jane's disappearance."

"Pete, I may have something that would help. When I met Germaine in Denver, I had a picture of Jane – an old glossy photograph – and I let Germaine hold it. Then, I put it back in my purse. I have it now in my desk. It would have my prints on it, of course, but maybe enough from Germaine that you could do a match?"

"That's a possibility. Can you try to touch it very little yourself and carefully wrap it in cotton and FedEx it to me? Send it to Columbus police headquarters, in care of Detective Carmine Cisneros. I'll let him to know expect it. "

"I'll get the envelope out to you first thing in the morning."

Then she brought up the other thing she wanted to ask him. "I know it's probably not important now, but do you think you could track down this Paul James? I don't think that however he and Jane were involved matters now, but it's a loose end. There's a limit, it seems, to what these commercial people search services can find. So, maybe with your resources you could track down what happened to him – and if there was or is a 'Mrs. James' still alive."

"Of course. And how old do you think he would be?"

"Well, from what Phyllis told me that she remembered of what Jane once told her, he wasn't more than a few years older than Jane. So maybe just under 80. I guess it could be a couple of years one way or the other."

"I'll start working on that immediately. I'm going to visit headquarters tomorrow and speak with Chief Murdock and Carmine about officially putting Jane's case back on active. And you got my message about my trip to Boston? Everything still all right with you for that?"

"Yes, fine. I've asked Roy if he can join us at some point. I'll have all my notes ready when we have our first lunch." She paused. "And I was thinking it might be easier to talk if we met at my place. So, please plan on lunch here, if that is all right with you. Then I think Roy might be able to come over for dinner."

"That's fine if it's not too much trouble for you. I'll send you a message sometime tomorrow to let you know what I'm finding out here about reopening the case."

She agreed and they signed off. Her martini glass was drained, but between the cocktail and the telephone conversation, she felt better than she had in days. "Maybe I'll avenge you, Jane," she said out loud. A memory of Jane in her classroom, with her heart-shaped smiling face, short blond hair and upright posture came to Zora. The light in the living room had died. "Just like Jane," she thought and felt the melancholy sinking in again.

CHAPTER TWENTY-THREE

The next morning, after Zora got back from the office supply store where she sent Jane's photograph via FedEx, the first phone call of the day came not from Pete or anyone in Denver but from Phyllis. Zora was drinking her second cup of coffee and scanning news on her computer. When she heard the familiar voice, she said, "Phyllis! What a pleasant surprise! How are you?"

The older woman sounded animated. "I'm doing well, Zora, as I hope you are. I've sent you my new book – it just came from the publishers. You don't have to tell me whether you like the poems or not!"

"But I'm sure I will. Thank you so much."

"And I did check on something else you asked me about. Our current building manager went back over the building security records from the time several weeks before Jane went missing. There were no reported intrusions, and there was no record of anyone being admitted who didn't have a key card. But Jane could have let someone in, or let that person use her key card for the front door. I just don't remember her saying anything about a visitor or visitors, but, of course, it's been a long time. As I told you before, however, some of her jewelry apparently went missing. I wish I knew that for certain, or whether she just gave it away to the charity auction."

"Phyllis, you're being very helpful. And I may be making some progress. Can I get back to you in a few days? I may have something to report!"

"Oh! That would be wonderful. I always felt you would find out what happened to Jane. And I hope we can see each other again, no matter what. I did enjoy your visit."

Zora felt a twinge of guilt. So many people counting on her, it seemed, to solve the mystery of Jane's death. And was she really any closer? Well, maybe. Especially if a positive match was made with Germaine's prints. But before learning if the prints matched, Zora wanted to jot down the other possible solutions to the crime.

The first one came easily: what if Mai had helped Murray do away with Jane? The motive could have been that Mai thought Jane's testimony would be so damning that he would get a long sentence. Or, perhaps, Mai had been jealous of Jane for some time and just wanted her out of the picture. Zora still had trouble seeing Jane in a romantic relationship with Murray, and he said there wasn't one. But he could easily be lying. And Jane had been unattached, had trusted him. He was good looking then and knew how to seduce women, maybe even Jane. Would all this add up to Mai's becoming an accomplice – or even acting alone? Zora could not rule it out.

The next possibility involved Hal Hubbard. Motive? Money, apparently, although she had heard conflicting evidence about whether Jane had left him much or not. Hal had said not; Brian had implied it was enough to help them buy their house in Princeton. "And money is often at the center of many crimes," she reminded herself. "The fact that I liked Hal and Brian should not influence me now."

Parch himself, of course, still had to be the prime suspect. Whether he worked with someone might become clearer if they identified Germaine as being involved. Zora's instincts after she met him told her that if he was responsible for Jane's death, he had not acted alone. He did not have a good alibi for that day, and he certainly had the best motive, but something didn't add up for her when she thought of him as a lone killer.

Then, there were the less probable scenarios. Could Phyllis somehow have been involved? What possible motive would she have had? For many years, she and Jane had been fast friends. Zora was not aware of any breaks in that friendship, much less any event that would have led to murder. Phyllis seemed well off. Could something as trivial as Phyllis' wanting Jane's jewelry even conceivably have led to a rift that led to murder? "I guess anything is possible, and I wasn't out there for many years," Zora reminded herself.

And what about Jane's alleged affair with Paul James? Had it even happened? Or had it possibly gone on longer than Jane had shared with Phyllis? Was there a jealous Mrs. James? Had she waited all those years between Jane's time in graduate school and retirement to plot – and then execute – a murder because of jealousy? This seemed the least likely of all the possible theories. "And yet, I have to track it down. Jealousy, like money, can be a powerful motive."

After another hour of revising what she wrote, she got up and walked around her living room. A light rain was falling outside; she decided to stay indoors. The question uppermost in her mind now was whether to call Germaine St. George. "For some reason, she wanted me to be notified that she was ill. Will she tell me any-thing over the phone?" While that seemed doubtful, Zora's internal voice was telling her to contact Germaine, without, of course, say-ing anything about her fingerprints. Finally, she found the number for Denver's Mt. Sinai Hospital and placed the call. The informa-tion desk connected her to the nurses' station on another floor. Knowing that they would likely not give out patient information to a stranger, Zora had planned what to say.

A male with a deep voice answered: "Ward Six, Lester Peakes speaking."

"Hello. My name is Zora Erickson. I am a friend of one of your patients, Germaine St. George, and I'm calling from Boston. I was notified yesterday that Mrs. St. George was admitted to your hos-pital. She had asked that I be contacted, and her resident building manager called me. I am wondering if she is able to accept calls and visitors or if you can give me any indication of her condition."

There was a notable pause. Had Lester temporarily muffled his receiver? Then, "I'm sorry but we cannot give out any information except to a patient's designated health surrogate. I can tell you that Mrs. St. George was taken back to intensive care this morn-ing." His tone softened. "I'm sorry that we cannot help you more. Please feel free to call back to speak with Mrs. St. George when she is able to have phone calls." He hung up.

Zora sat back, feeling frustrated. Maybe in a day or two Ger-maine could talk? "Or be dead?" Zora thought with mixed feelings of regret and anger. "I feel like I'm so close to something and it isn't working out." Even if Germaine's prints could be lifted and matched with a set from Jane's car, that did not make her a mur-derer – or even an accomplice. But maybe they could confront Murray Parch with the evidence?

Zora's cell phone pinged – the text message was from Pete. "Call me when you can – anytime today." She dialed immediately.

"I sent off the photograph this morning for next day delivery," she reported, as soon as he answered.

"Well, I have something for you, and I have a question. First, Carmine has checked with the Chief, and we are reopening the case. Now, my question. I've been working on finding your Mr. James. Carmine agreed that we could query the FBI's date base if we don't find anything with our resources. No one with that name and fitting the description you gave me is apparently anywhere in the US, including in or out of prison. And no one deceased in the last twenty years fits, either. We will request FBI resources to expand the search to Mexico and Canada. So, my question is: do you, by any chance, know the maiden name of James' wife? It's possible she might have divorced him at some point and taken back her own name."

Zora sighed. "No, I have no idea, Pete. I've found out so little about Paul James, and I doubt there is anyone now who would know about his wife. I can contact Professor Armillato again, I guess. I'll do that and get back to you. Was there anything else?"

"No." Then a pause. She wondered if he was debating what to say. Was he holding something back from her? Then, "I'll get back to you if we find out anything – and, of course, as soon as we get that photograph and do the fingerprint match. If you think of anything else that I should know, text me or call. I'll be home all evening." His tone actually sounded less impersonal, she thought, and was encouraged.

Zora had one more idea about the mysterious Paul James. "If he taught art, maybe he has published. I should at least be able to find that out." After Googling several topics, including "Southwestern Art.", articles about "Art Critics," and "Contemporary American Art," she finally found one reference under "Artists of the Southwest." The referenced article, an extensive critique of four artists, had three authors, one of whom was listed as a "P. James". It had been published fifteen years ago in a scholarly journal with which Zora was not familiar, but the article was available on line. The full names of all three authors were listed, as were their scholarly affiliations. Paul James was listed second, and under his name appeared the words, "University of Toronto." Zora's felt a jolt of energy. She read the article hurriedly and found it mildly interesting, although it reviewed the work of artists she did not know. When she finished, she sent a text to Pete: "Try Toronto. Found a reference to Paul James there from fifteen years ago."

She looked at her watch. She was due to meet a friend at Boston College to attend a jazz quartet program at five. But first, she wanted to see if the University of Toronto listed their faculty on line. After she scrolled through their somewhat confusing web site in order to find out in what division or department art history was taught, she did find a listing of faculty, including "Professors Emeriti." There, the third name listed was "P. James, Ph.D., USC." At the bottom of the column, a phone number for the "Department of Art History" was listed. Her call to that number only reached an answering machine. She debated about leaving a message, and then decided it would be better to have this conversation in person. Plus, Pete might uncover something that would be more helpful. She could wait until the next day. And, after all, if Germaine's fingerprints on the photograph matched a set from Jane's car, they would be off on a much more productive line of investigation.

* * *

For two days now, no one had answered the phone – not the land line or the cell. "She's not like that" was the first thought, but obviously she was – or something was wrong. She was the only one to count on, and now she couldn't be reached. She was supposed to stop Zora Erickson. Had she done that? How to find out? Had she betrayed the plan? That couldn't be allowed to happen.

CHAPTER TWENTY-FOUR

Zora spent the next morning at the dentist. She had planned to call the Art History department when she got home, but she felt tired and decided to take a short nap. Then, at 1:45 p.m., Pete called. Zora had been prepared for the worst, but from the moment he said her name, she knew something had changed.

"Zora, we have a match. One set of prints on your photo matches one set from Jane's car."

"Are you sure?"

" There are three sets of prints on the photo. One set is Jane's – we've had hers on file since the case started. I'm assuming the second set is yours, because that set does not match anything we found in Jane's car, so the third set must be Germaine's. Unless there was still somebody else who handled that photo."

"Not that I know of. Of course Jane could have shown it to someone else before she sent it to me. What are you going to do next?" She tried to keep her voice steady. Her arms tingled.

"If it's possible, we're going to go out to Colorado and interview Germaine. The prints alone don't prove she had anything to do with Jane's death, but it may be an important lead. She told you she had never met Jane, but clearly she at least was in her car. Have you heard anything more about Germaine's condition?"

"No. I could call the hospital, but I guess they'd be more likely to talk with you or one of your people."

"Yes, that's probably right. Although Germaine might be more willing to talk with you if she's in any condition to talk with anybody. I'll find out from Carmine how he wants to conduct the interview. It's probably going to be an official visit, but would you come along if Carmine authorizes it?"

Zora had anticipated this question. She thought of Germaine St. George, weak, ill, lying in a hospital bed, being interviewed by the police about her possible role in a murder nearly thirteen years ago. She remembered her own visit with Germaine. She had neither liked nor disliked her, but she had felt Germaine was withholding something. "I'd like to be there if I could and if you think that would help."

"Then I'll talk with Carmine and we'll decide how quickly we can move on this. As soon as I know the plan, I'll call you." He paused. "If this interferes with my trip to Boston, we may have to reschedule – if we still need to meet."

Did she detect a slight note of regret in his voice? She quieted her imagination. This was business. "Yes, of course. Germaine may mean a break through."

"I'll call you as soon as we have the schedule nailed down."

After Pete rang off, Zora thought about calling Mt. Sinai again to inquire about Germaine's condition but finally reconciled with herself that the Columbus police were not likely to want her along on the trip, even if perhaps Pete wouldn't mind. Shifting her attention, she pulled up the phone number for the University of Toronto's Art History Department office.

This time, a pleasant female voice answered. "This is Joy Davis. May I help you?"

"Thank you, Ms. Davis. My name is Zora Erickson. I'm a retired teacher, and I'm trying to track down an acquaintance who may have been on your faculty some years ago. His name is Paul James."

"Dr. James? Yes, he was with us for a number of years. I came into the department twelve years ago, and I think he retired about two years later. We do see him now and then, at Art Museum events -- you know, we have a wonderful museum here. We're not allowed to give out the private phone numbers for faculty, but I could give you his email address. He still uses his university account."

"That would be very helpful - thank you," Zora replied, trying not to sound too eager.

There was a short pause. "Here we are." Joy Davis read off the email address. "I miss seeing Dr. James. He and his lovely wife have always been so gracious and interested in everything in our department."

Zora's heart skipped a beat. "I don't recall his wife's first name. Is she still alive?"

"Evangeline? Well, she was the last time I saw them – maybe about six months ago now. If Dr. James comes in or I see him, do you want me to tell him you are trying to contact him?"

Zora thought fast. "No, please don't bother. It's been many years, and he may not remember me, so I wouldn't want to embarrass him. But I will drop him a note. Thank you so much. You have been very helpful."

So his wife was alive. "At least, he has *a* wife now who is alive." Zora realized that this could be a later wife than the one Paul James cheated on with Jane – if, indeed, that affair even happened.

But all this seemed beside the point now. Zora's instincts told her that the key to finding out what happened to Jane clearly lay with Germaine St. George. "Maybe she was lying about not ever having met Jane, but that doesn't mean she killed her – or helped Murray kill her." Zora was pacing around her living room. "But if she had nothing to do with Jane's death, why did she lie about knowing her? She could just have said she went to Ohio to try to persuade Jane not to testify against Murray."

Her phone beeped. The text message was from Pete. It read, "Check your email. Info on P James."

The email was brief. "Found a Paul James in Toronto, Canada. His profile seems to match the information you gave me." There followed a street address in the Yorkville section. Zora texted back: "Read your email. Thanks. Any information about his having a wife at that address? First name possibly 'Evangeline'?" His return text was immediate: "Will check that. Talk to you later. May know more about Denver."

It seemed as if there was nothing more Zora could do at the moment, so she made herself a small vegetable salad for lunch and went for a brisk walk afterwards. Her mouth had stopped hurting from the morning's dental procedure, the sun was shining, and she met one of her favorite neighbors who joined her. All in all, the afternoon was shaping up well.

Pete called her two hours later. "Here's my afternoon report," he said in a businesslike tone. "Yes, there is an Evangeline James listed at the same address as Paul. They have an unlisted land line phone but I got the number." He read it to her.

She wrote it down and asked him to continue.

"Carmine is working with the Denver police to set up a meeting with Germaine St. George. As of this afternoon, she is still in intensive care, with her condition described as 'stable' but one of the detectives out there was able to speak to the hospitalist, who said she might be able to be interviewed for a short time in a few days. So, Carmine wants to fly out there Saturday or Sunday and do the interview on Monday of next week."

"Do you need me to come?"

"Carmine doesn't object, so if you want to come, yes, but they may not let us see her for long, and we'll have to do the formal interview first. I should know the trip plans by later tonight. I can email you the details as soon as I have them."

"Thanks, Pete. I'll think some more about it. Maybe I should make a later trip to see her, after the police do their part."

"Whatever you decide is fine with me." He hesitated. Then, "You've done good work by finding out about her."

Zora smiled to herself. A compliment from Pete at last! "I *will* think about it."

Very late that night, Pete sent her the trip itinerary for himself and Carmine Cisneros. They would arrive in Denver mid-day on Sunday and leave late on Monday night. Zora looked up flights from Boston and found she could very nearly match their schedule. But she hesitated. Something was telling her not to make a reservation yet. She decided to sleep on it.

She was in bed with the lights out when her land line phone rang. Without turning on the light, she reached for the receiver. Roy had told her a dozen times to get caller ID, but since she primarily used her cell phone, and most people called her on that, she only had the ID feature there. When she picked up, no one spoke. She could sense that the line was open. "Pete?" she said, thinking that he might be on his cell phone which could cause a slight delay. Silence. She thought she heard breathing. And then a voice, muffled, sounding far away, not clearly male or female, said "stop now", and the line went dead. Zora lay wide awake for an hour, and then she drifted into a troubled sleep. In it, someone in a large, black car was following her, but she could never see who it was.

CHAPTER TWENTY-FIVE

Roy stopped in for coffee the next morning, and Zora gave him an update on the case. She did not tell him about the late night phone call, because she had made up her mind: she was going with Pete to Denver, and she didn't want to hear any nonsense like "no travel while you're in danger". She did tell him that Pete and Carmine Cisneros were making the trip, emphasizing how much she trusted Pete and how important the visit to Germaine could be.

"Mom, I'm still going to worry about you, but I know you will be careful. Will you promise to check in with me every day?" He almost told her that he would hold Pete responsible for her safety, but he knew this would anger her. And he did trust her judgment. Instead, he said, "You remember that I'm taking Kressida and the kids to Disney World next week. We'll leave Monday and come back the next Sunday. I think Kress is looking forward to it more than the kids - no cooking for seven days!" Zora chuckled, secretly relieved that his mind would be on a few other things than worrying about what she was doing. "Well, good, and you'll be back just in time for Pete Le Gall's visit." Roy noted the lightness in her voice when she said this.

Just before he left her house, she gave him two envelopes. "Cards for the kids with a little something in them so they can buy things that you and Kressida probably wouldn't buy for them!" she told him gaily. "I hope you all really have a good time."

He gave her a hug and kiss on his way out. He looked back at her waving to him on her porch. "I wonder if something could happen between Mom and Pete," he thought, realizing that maybe this was a little far fetched. His memory of Pete was of a serious, hardened detective, certainly not a romantic figure. "But he was a nice guy to work with." As much as Roy knew how deeply his parents had been in love, he found he was not disappointed at the idea Zora could find someone new.

* * *

Zora gave some thought about whether to initiate contact with Paul James, but she had no idea how she would go about doing that. Write to him and say, "You don't know me, but your wife could be a suspect in the death of a good friend of mine and I'd like to talk to her." Not exactly! Perhaps if the meeting with Germaine didn't resolve everything it would be useful to continue pursuing other leads, but right now that didn't seem like a priority.

Pete called her at noon. "You OK?" he asked, and for a minute Zora wondered if he had some sixth sense about the phone call she had gotten the night before. She had decided not to tell him about it until they were in Denver together. After all, it wasn't as if she was being threatened with some specific harm. At least not at the moment.

"Fine! Roy was here a little while ago. He's not thrilled with the idea of my going to Denver with the police on official business, but I think he trusts you to look after me."

Pete gave a deep laugh. "So you've decided to go! Not sure you need any looking after, but I do understand about children worrying about their parents. My daughter calls me several times a week!"

They reviewed the travel schedule and agreed to meet at the Brown Palace for dinner Sunday night. "I assume you haven't heard anything more about Germaine's condition from Mt. Sinai?" Zora asked.

"No, and I don't expect to unless there is some change and the hospital won't let us talk with her. I hope that doesn't happen."

"Are you going to put any kind of surveillance on Parch now?" Zora was curious.

"Not yet. We don't have enough evidence even to tie Germaine to the murder, let alone Parch, but after this weekend we may. I'll check in with you again tomorrow. I'm golfing in a Y tournament most of the day, but I'll be free after four."

"Good! I'll be packing. I've checked the weather out there. It's supposed to be warm and maybe a little windy. Have a good time tomorrow." Zora realized that she did need to think about what to wear on the trip to Denver. "What is appropriate for a police interview with a suspect in a murder case?" she wondered, and then laughed at herself. Could this be the occasion for a little shopping? She had all day Saturday. Maybe Ellie would join her? She put in a call to her, and the answer was an enthusiastic "yes!" Ellie would come to the townhouse and they would take the "T" downtown from there.

* * *

After the shopping trip and lunch at Durgin Park on Saturday, Ellie came back with Zora to the townhouse since she had left her car there. "I love the shoes you bought!" she told Zora, as they admired the very red, very shiny patent leather pumps with a bow on each one. "And yours, too," Zora told Ellie, who looked vaguely disgusted. "Oh, I guess they are all right. Sensible shoes for a pregnant lady." She looked down at the suede loafers with the rubber heels. "At least Tyler will approve of them."

They settled down on the patio for iced tea and one oatmeal cookie each. "I've only gained ten pounds, which the doctor said is good," Ellie admitted. "But I'm hungry all the time. I try to eat celery, but I miss your baking!"

"I'll pack up some cookies for you to take home – you can pretend they're for Tyler. That way, you won't feel so guilty when you have one. Or two."

After Ellie left, Zora checked her cell phone. She had deliberately left it off all morning, knowing Pete was busy and that if Roy needed her, he would call again. When she turned it on she saw the "called missed" notice and checked the number. It was from a 303 exchange, and she thought she remembered the number as Christine Kelly's. She hit the "call" key.

"This is Christine. Is this Mrs. Erickson?'

"It is, Christine. I've had my phone off. Do you have some news about Mrs. St. George?"

The pause was long enough that Zora knew what she was going to hear before Christine said it. "Mrs. Erickson, I'm so sorry, but Mrs. St. George died early this morning. The hospital called us at 8 a.m. I tried to call you after that as soon as I could."

Surprising herself, Zora felt a lump come to her throat. "Thank you for thinking of me, Christine. Was it her heart?"

"Yes. She'd been back in intensive care and they said she suffered a massive attack. I guess there was nothing they could do."

"Have you notified her niece and nephew?"

"I've left messages for them to call me. I want to talk with them personally. I will ask them to come here and take her things. I also have to go to the hospital and take home the things she had there."

Suddenly Zora remembered. "Christine, I'm very grateful you thought to call me. This is very sad. But there is one favor I would like to ask. When you bring Germaine's things back to her apartment, would you, please, see if she took a framed picture with her to the hospital, and if not, is there one in the drawer of her bedside table? It will be of a man, perhaps her late husband. I think you said you had seen something on that table that then wasn't there the morning she went to the hospital."

"Yes, I will do that. Is it a picture you would like to have? I would have to get permission from her family to let you have it, I guess. But I could ask."

"It's not so important that I have the actual picture, but if you could take a shot of it with your cell phone and email that to me, I would be grateful. It will answer a question about Germaine that I never had the chance to ask her."

"I will let you know. And about the funeral arrangements. She was such a nice lady, a strong person, I always thought. We will miss her. And I'm sorry for your loss. You were her friend."

"Yes. Well, thank you again for being so considerate. You can text me the picture or email it to me." Zora read out her email address. "If the niece or nephew wants to talk with me, you can give them my contacts." Privately, Zora could not imagine that they would be interested in reaching her at all, but it sounded like the right thing to tell Christine Kelly.

As soon as she ended the conversation, she looked at her watch. It was 3:30 p.m. Pete should be calling sometime after 4:00. Nevertheless, she sent him a text: "Very urgent. Need to talk."

Zora was too agitated to sit, so she picked up a sweater and went out her front door. The neighborhood was quiet. She began walking toward the Charles River. "What can we do now?" she asked herself, unconsciously including Pete in the "we". "The finger prints mean she was with Jane at some point, but maybe well before that Saturday. Maybe she did come east to ask Jane not to testify against Murray, or maybe he asked her to come and help disappear Jane. We may never know – unless Murray can be broken down and give a confession."

And what if it was someone else altogether who was with Jane that last day? Who was in the car with Jane - if, in fact, Mrs. Elijah's account was accurate? It could have been a man; it could have been a man dressed as a woman. But she had gone over all this before. Zora felt her frustration rising. She walked faster. After half an hour, she turned back toward the townhouse. She hadn't come to any new realizations, but Pete might call at any minute, and she didn't want to have that conversation while walking around Cambridge.

CHAPTER TWENTY-SIX

He called at 4:30. "I just got home. Saw you message when I came off the course. What's up? Are you all right?"

"Pete, I'm fine, but I had a call from Denver. Germaine died this morning. Maybe the hospital is trying to notify you and Carmine."

"Damn! No, I haven't heard anything yet. Who called you?"

"Christine Kelly, one of the supervisors at Carter-by-the-Lake, where Germaine lived. She's the one who called me originally to tell me Germaine was in the hospital."

"And I suppose Ms. Kelly hadn't talked with Germaine or anything in the last twenty-four hours?"

"I don't think so, although she didn't say. She's getting in touch with Germaine's niece and nephew. They live in Chicago and Brooklyn. Germaine only mentioned them to me briefly, and I don't even know their names."

She could hear Pete sigh. "OK. Well, this isn't good news. I'll get in touch with Carmine. We'll cancel our trip. Carmine's already said he wants to interview Parch again, in light of Germaine's finger prints in Jane's car and Parch's history with Germaine. That's about all we have to go on now."

"I know. I'm sorry about this. I wish I had had more time with her when I visited and that I had thought of better questions. You remember that I told you I saw a picture by Germaine's bed but couldn't see who was in it? From what Christine told me, Germaine either slipped the picture into her bed stand drawer or took it with her to the hospital. I've asked Christine to try to find the picture and take a photograph of it and text or email it to me. If it is of Murray, that might give you something to tie them more closely together – and to Jane's disappearance."

"Yes, that's a possibility. Let me know when you get something from this Christine and if it's of Parch."

"Pete, because of all this and if you and Carmine are going to see Parch, are you still planning to come to Boston a week from Monday?" Zora tried to keep her tone neutral and businesslike.

"So far, yes. I'll call Carmine. I know this sets us back, but don't worry; we're going to find out what happened to Jane. We're not going to let this go. And I still think you and I need to talk in person. I may be able to jog your memory if we do that. Can I let you know for certain by tomorrow?"

After the call, Zora logged on and cancelled her own airline reservation for Denver. She couldn't get a refund on the ticket, but she did have ninety days to book another trip at an equivalent (or higher) fare for only fifty dollars more. "Maybe I should go back to Columbus," she speculated. At one point, she had thought about trying to find and interview other former clients of Parch. But Pete would be visiting her in just over a week. "Time to plan a trip to Columbus later if we don't get this solved the way we are going."

And then she had a thought. "I've had some luck calling on people 'cold' during this investigation. And I have time to myself next week, before Pete visits, and Roy will be away so he won't be checking up on me in person. Maybe I should go to Toronto to see if meeting Paul James and his wife will be anything but a dead end."

She checked the flight schedules for Toronto. It was an easy, non-stop trip from Boston. Flights were available every one of the next eight days. She could exchange her cancelled ticket for one to Toronto. "I'd better sleep on it," she told herself.

She fixed herself some warmed over veal stew and watched two hours of a PBS program on badgers that she completely forgot about an hour after she had seen it. She sat in the dark for with the television off, calmer than she had been earlier. She checked her phone. Nothing from Christine. Or anyone else. She wondered in an almost detached way if she would get a threatening phone call tonight. She realized she had never told Pete about the call on Thursday night. But by the time she went to bed, neither of her phones had rung. She turned off her cell phone and plugged it into the charger. Fifteen minutes later, a text message came in from Christine Kelly, but Zora was fast asleep.

CHAPTER TWENTY-SEVEN

Take a shower, make coffee, boil two eggs, pick up the *Boston Globe* from the delivery box. Her Sunday morning routine. Thinking hard about whether to take the trip to Toronto. Trying to remember anything new that she could about her visit with Germaine that could be useful to the police. Finally, Zora remembered to turn on her cell phone. The usual vendor messages appeared. Nothing from Roy, or her daughter, or Pete. But an email from Christine Kelly with an attachment. Zora poured herself a cup of coffee and sat down at her kitchen table.

Christine's message was straightforward: "I found a framed picture in the drawer by Germaine's bed. It was the only one there. She has lots of pictures all over the apartment, so I don't know if she used to move them around. But I did take a photo of the one in the drawer. It is attached. I'm still waiting to hear from her niece and nephew. I will let you know about any memorial service or anything else they plan. Thank you for being a good friend to Germaine. We will miss her."

Zora clicked on the attachment. She enlarged it to its maximum size. Then she sat perfectly still, not touching the phone on the table in front of her, and looked at the picture. Not a formal portrait but a three-quarters shot, probably taken by someone at a casual event. Despite all her sorrow, frustration, and anger at Jane's disappearance, Zora's first thought was "Germaine was loyal all this time." Of course, the picture by itself still didn't prove anything definitively, but it was a link. She let herself feel a moment of intense anger at Germaine, but that passed. "She did what she thought she had to do."

And now Zora knew what *she* needed to do, without Pete or Roy or the police, without anyone else. She would bring them in later, but she had to know, first, if she held the final key. Was she in any danger? Possibly, but she felt strangely calm. She needed some information before she could take another step. She found Hal's cell phone number and texted him two questions, saying he could call her if he preferred. In twenty minutes, he texted back, and she was not surprised at his answers. He offered to talk with her, but she replied that she would do that later. The net was tightening.

The next step might involve a short trip to a place Zora was familiar with. But now, as she sat at her desk, she needed to make a crucial decision. Should she send a message before her visit? But if she did, would she be welcome? "Probably not!" And yet, she did not want the trip to be a waste of time. Finally, she made her decision. She would call. If she reached an answering machine, she would leave a well rehearsed message. If someone answered, she would say the same thing, leaving no time for a reply and just hang up. She wrote out in long hand what she was going to say and then practiced saying it out loud.

Finally, she picked up her smart phone and punched in the number she was calling. After four rings, a synthetic voice came on the line. "No one is available to answer this call. Please leave a message after the tone."

"This is Zora Erickson. Germaine has died. I want to talk with you. I will meet you in the park with the fountain near you tomorrow at 2 p.m. I will be alone. Call this number by six tonight if you cannot meet me." She ended the message by reciting her cell phone number.

To prevent having to talk with Pete and forestall any questions, she sent him a text. "Am visiting a friend in Newton today and staying over with her. Will call you tomorrow."

Ten hours to go until her 6 p.m. deadline. Zora decided to make an airline reservation for an early morning flight on Monday. If she received a call back before 6 p.m., she could always cancel the reservation.

To keep herself busy, she cleaned out her storage closet and sewed buttons on two blouses she had been neglecting for weeks. She wrote a short email to Ellie and Tyler, saying that she was taking a break from her "investigation" and would be spending some time with friends, including one from Columbus who would be visiting her in a week and whom she would like to invite them over to meet. She cleaned out her freezer and baked two loaves of rye bread. She checked television news occasionally, but not much of interest was going on in the world. By 5:30 p.m., no one had called. At 5:45 p.m., her cell phone rang. She jumped and then looked at the calling number. Roy.

"Hi, Mom. Just wanted to check in. We're here in Florida. The kids are enjoying the swimming pool and Kress and I are going to join them by the pool for a glass of something. What are you up to?"

"Just a lazy Sunday at home, honey. Don't worry about me. I think I'll do some shopping tomorrow, maybe see Ellie. Give Kressida a hug for me and enjoy your week. You can tell me all about it when you get back."

"Will do, Mom. Is Pete still planning to come next week?"

"As far as I know. I'll have you all over for dinner. We'll talk when you get back." She looked at her watch: 5:48 p.m. "I have bread in the oven, so I'm going to ring off now. Love you, Roy."

"Love you, too, Mom."

No missed calls had come in while she was talking with Roy. At 6:05, she poured herself a glass of Merlot. She was sitting down again in front of the TV when her cell phone beeped. A text message. She held her breath and opened the message. Three words: "Will be there". The sending number was unfamiliar to her, but, of course, it was from a cell phone, and a number she had not seen previously. She felt a sense of relief and at the same time her adrenalin was overcoming the sedative effects of the wine. "Well, I'm into it now," she told herself.

One more thing to do. She sent a text to Pete: "Turning in early. Hope your day was good. I'm staying an extra day with my friend but will call you Tuesday." Before sending the text, Zora thought hard about whether she should reveal to him the purpose of her trip and what she hoped to find out before he and Carmine visited Parch. But, after all, she really had no new information at this point. Better to proceed with her plan and let them proceed with theirs.

After a light supper, she went to bed at 9 p.m., setting set her alarm for 4 a.m. Sleep came, but not without dreams – one was of a body in a lake and with a disembodied voice saying, "that's her."

CHAPTER TWENTY-EIGHT

Zora's flight left Logan Airport at 7:15 a.m. After it landed, she took a taxi directly to her hotel, where they allowed her an early check-in. Once settled, she unpacked her few things and took a thirty-minute nap. Refreshed, she showered, dressed and decided to have a light lunch in the lobby restaurant.

One cup of tomato soup and a toasted cheese and ham sandwich later, she noted that it was 1:15 p.m. She signed for the meal and left. The day was warm and heating up. She put on sunglasses. She reached in the pocket of her purse for her phone; no new messages. She put it back. Four blocks to the park. Normally, she would have enjoyed the walk but today her mind was so filled with questions – and what she should or should not say – that she hardly noticed the flowering almond bushes lining the boulevard or the occasional pots of petunias along her route. As she came to the park, she recognized the pine grove and the prairie flowers. Several benches ringed the fountain, where two small children were playing with a model boat. The mothers chatted nearby. It was 1:45 p.m. Zora sat down on a bench where she could see anyone coming up any of the paths. Her arms tingled and her heart rate increased as she told herself, firmly, to be calm.

She saw him first, coming up the north path, walking slowly, using a cane. For a fleeting second, Zora thought that maybe she had been inconsiderate, choosing a place that was difficult to get to. She had selected the park partly for her own safety – somewhere that she could call for help or get away if it came to that. These thoughts vanished when Zora saw the shorter woman with the wavy white hair walking a step behind him, just touching his arm. Zora stood as they approached. They saw her. A flood of emotions nearly swamped Zora – relief, joy, triumph and even a touch of anger. For a second, no one moved. Then Zora reached out both hands, which were surprisingly steady. "Hello, Jane," she said.

Paul James continued toward Zora and the bench. He nodded at her and sat down. But Jane came directly to Zora and grasped her hands, holding them for a second and then dropping them to look searchingly at Zora. "You're looking well. You found me," she said in the voice Zora remembered. Warm, low, assured.

"Yes. And Germaine kept your secret all these years."

"Did she suffer at the end? I tried to call her several days ago, and she wasn't answering. That was not like her."

"It was her heart. I think she had good care. I had planned to visit her again, but I did not understand until she died what had been going on. She kept a picture of you by her bed. That was how I finally knew."

Jane looked past Zora at something invisible, something only she could see. Then she gathered herself. "I would like you to meet my husband, Paul James." He stood up to shake Zora's hand rather formally. "Mrs. Erickson, you have come a long way. And you have been very concerned about my wife. I thank you for that." Zora nodded, not quite sure how to respond, but she said, "And I am pleased to meet Jamie." She saw the look of surprise and then amusement in his eyes.

"Paul, do you mind if Zora and I take a short walk around the park and leave you here for just a few moments?" It was a question, but Zora knew Jane didn't really need an answer.

"Of course, dear. I'll enjoy the rest." His smile was infectious. Jane took Zora's arm and they started down the south path.

After walking a few yards, Jane stopped, turned toward Zora and gave her a long look. ""When did you first suspect?"

"I didn't, not for a long time. I thought you were dead. For a long time, I thought that either Murray had killed you or he had someone else do it – and that person might have been Germaine. She left finger prints in your car. But the police couldn't identify them until just recently when I remembered I had a glossy photo of you that I had shared with Germaine. She handled it and left prints. The thing was, I could never quite see her as a murderer. I met with Murray. He's not well. I didn't like him, but I also had trouble seeing him as someone who had killed."

They resumed their walk. Jane was silent for a few seconds.

"Were there others you suspected?"

"Oh, yes. Murray's wife, Mai. Your second cousin, Hal, who, by the way, has been very helpful. It was he who confirmed that your mother's maiden name was Evangeline McCall, and that he found Canadian coins in your dresser drawer, along with some others from foreign countries."

"Is he still with his friend, Brian? Did you visit them?"

"He is – they are married now. I spent a pleasant afternoon and evening with them. I think Hal took good care of the rest of your money, although he and Brian may have spent some of it on their house in Princeton."

"I hope so. And I left him all my books – except, of course, for the ones I could not part with."

"I have your list of the books. Some titles were erased. Are those the ones you brought here?"

"Yes. Anything Jamie had written in, anything he had recommended, those I brought with me."

"But you brought your copy of Jane Austen's 'Sense and Sensibility', too, didn't you? When I looked at Hal's library, he had all your Jane Austen books – except that one. I guess I should have figured out that that was a clue."

Jane smiled. "Yes, I suppose that was foolish of me, but Ms. Austen has always been my favorite, and I loved teaching that book."

They approached the entrance to the park and took another path toward the pine grove.

"How did you know about this place?" Jane asked, turning to look at Zora.

"Rashad and I came to Toronto several times on buying trips. On the first one, we discovered Yorkville and loved it. We came to this park together a couple of times. But the area has changed so much. All the international stores. I hardly recognize it."

"And you found us, here in Toronto. How?"

"Once or twice you said the name 'Jamie' to Phyllis. And you told her you had a romance with a professor in graduate school. That he was married at the time, so you broke it off. It took some work, but I was able to find out who Jamie was – or at least I was pretty sure. The detective who investigated your case in Columbus after you disappeared has been very helpful. As has my son, Roy, who is also with the police." Zora stopped, not knowing exactly how to tell the next part delicately. "I thought that maybe if Jamie had a wife who was still jealous of you after all these years, she might have found out where you were and come after you. I'm sorry for having that suspicion."

"She died fifteen years ago. After our affair, she and Jamie did reconcile. Jamie and I had not been in touch since Illinois but he tracked me down. He had moved here to Toronto and was teaching at the university. I visited him here several times after that. We fell in love again, almost as if we had never been apart. When I decided to set up my death, I knew I wanted to come here, to be with him. Mother's passport had not expired, so I used that to set up my new identity as 'Evangeline McCall'. Until you started investigating, I don't think anyone but Germaine knew."

She paused. There was a bench in front of them. Suddenly Zora was feeling a little tired. "Shall we sit down for a minute?"

They sat and remained silent for a few seconds. Then Zora asked the one question she still could not completely answer for herself: "Why did you do it?"

Jane did not turn away from Zora's gaze. "Because I wanted Murray Parch to suffer. Mother had died several years before I retired. Julia Lefkowitz had killed herself – I know he drove her to it. First she fell in love with him, he led her on, and then he swindled her. I loved Julia, not in a romantic way, but we grew very close. When she died, something in my mind changed. I thought that if I testified against Parch for what he did to me, how he took my money, he would get off very lightly. Because it was just financial fraud, not anything more serious. I *was* planning to testify. But then I began to think that if it looked as if he had murdered me – or had me killed – they might give him a much longer sentence. And that judge, the one who went on to become a state Supreme Court justice, did just that. Of course, if they'd found my actual dead body, the sentence might have been much worse – but I didn't want to go that far." She gave a dry laugh.

"And how did Germaine figure in all this?"

"After the news came out that I had been swindled, Germaine found me and called. She told me Parch had also swindled her. She had dropped charges against him, but she was regretting it since she now knew he was apparently cheating others. She asked if we could meet, and I agreed. I think that at first she must have been ambivalent, because deep down perhaps she still loved him. Did you sense that when you met her?"

"I couldn't tell. Her story was complicated. I met other people in Denver who seemed to think she had a sustained romantic relationship with Murray, and he admitted as much to me when I interviewed him."

"Yes, well, by the time Germaine and I talked, and I told her about Julia, she asked what I was going to do. Of course, I told her I had been planning to testify against Murray. But I had also by that time been thinking about staging my fake death and I told her that. I thought that the worst that could happen was that she would go to the police – or even tell Parch – in which case, I wouldn't have disappeared, and I would have denied telling her anything."

Jane brushed away a fly that had landed on her sleeve.

"After I went to see her in Denver, we talked some more and in the end, she offered to help. I had a few things to do before I disappeared, and I did need someone to help me with the details. She met me at the nursing home that day and drove me to the airport. Later, she shipped a few things to me – including the books I wanted to have. I had given her the key to my apartment. I was already 'Evangeline McCall' by the time I got on the plane in Columbus. We arranged that she would leave my car in the parking lot of that drugstore. And she would leave false clues – ashes in the ash tray - at the time, she smoked - a tissue with lipstick that obviously wasn't mine. It worked."

"That picture you sent to me with your Christmas card before you disappeared – it looked like you were sitting by a lake. Who took that? Was it Germaine?"

"Yes, when I visited her. It was on the grounds of the place where she had moved to."

"She asked me to drive her to that lake when I met her. I guess that was her way of giving me a hint about you, but, of course, I didn't dream of how you and she were really connected."

"What made you think Germaine might have been involved in my disappearance?

"You didn't give Mrs. Elijah her chocolates that last Saturday. She remembered that and that 'a lady with big hands' was in your car with you. I don't think she would make a very credible witness in a court room, but I believed her."

"Oh, dear. Ruth Elijah. I even bought the usual candy bars for her, but I was so preoccupied that I forgot to give them to her."

"But didn't you ever think about coming back? After all, Murray did serve time. And it wasn't as though they were going to find your 'dead body' and send him back to jail!"

"Yes, I have thought about it. But, you see, if the State of Ohio knew that Murray did not kill me or at least contribute to my 'death', they might compensate him for some of his time in prison. And he would come off as some type of innocent victim. From what Germaine has told me, his life is not a happy one, and for that I am very glad."

"He and Mai are divorced. She seems like a decent person. She lives in Florida and is able to work from her home. I think it was his lying to her, especially about all the other women, that made her leave him. Although I did suspect early on that maybe she had something to do with your 'death'. It wasn't clear when I met her whether she was closely in touch with Murray or not. He's been ill and appears to have a heart condition now. He looks old."

"I liked Mai. The three of us socialized when Murray was my broker and before I knew that he had swindled me. I feel badly that she had to be married to him, but I'm glad that she is on her own."

"Was it Germaine who sent me the 'stop' note? And who called me to say that?"

Jane took Zora's hand in hers and squeezed it gently. "Yes, it was Germaine who sent the note. She put it in a sealed envelope and then sent that envelope in another one to her niece in Brooklyn and asked her to mail the original. And I was the one who called you, but I had Paul say the words. I'm very sorry about that now. We must have frightened you, and that was wrong. I wanted you to think it was Parch who was threatening you."

Jane looked down at the pine needles under her feet. "You must understand, Zora, that I hated him. I still do. Anything to make his life miserable, anything to make him pay for all the harm he caused to so many people, not just me, but especially Julia, I was willing to do. And then, I started another life here in Toronto, with Jamie. Germaine kept me informed of whether anyone was still looking for me, whether I had been found out. And there never was any news. Until you came along."

She got up. "Let's start back. I don't want Jamie to worry. If you're staying over in Toronto, maybe you would be willing to come back to our apartment and we could finish talking there?"

"Yes. I can do that." They started back along the path toward the fountain.

Suddenly, Jane stopped. She faced Zora. "So, you know why I have done what I did. What about you, Zora? Why did you start looking for me? It was a long time ago."

"We were friends. Phyllis, who is very fond of you, never forgot you, either. I have a young friend who looked for her mother's killer for many years. It took her some time and put her in danger, but she persisted. I admired that. She has been a role model, of sorts. When I thought about you, I didn't want you to be lying in at the bottom of a lake somewhere or in a dirt pile with no one ever knowing what happened to you. I guess, to be honest, I wouldn't want that to happen to me."

Jane nodded. "I've caused you a great deal of effort. I did not want to be found, but you persisted." Zora could not tell if this was a form of thanks for her efforts or a rebuke.

They continued their walk in silence until the fountain came in sight. Jamie was still sitting on the bench. He struggled to his feet and smiled broadly when he saw them. Zora glimpsed the handsome young man he must have been – and still was, despite the white hair and slightly stooped appearance.

Jane kissed him lightly on the cheek. "I've invited Zora back to our apartment."

He nodded, "good", and the three of them began their slow procession out of the park.

CHAPTER TWENTY-NINE

Zora had arranged to meet them in the park because it was safe for her and close to where they lived. The neighborhood consisted of tasteful townhouses and low-rise apartment buildings. The James apartment, on the second floor of a red brick neo-colonial building, was decorated in warm colors of russet and gold. Original art – original as far as Zora could tell – hung on every wall.

"Please take any chair," Paul offered as Jane disappeared into the kitchen to make tea. Zora chose one with a view of the tree-lined boulevard outside. "Jane tells me that you and your late husband collected African art and other native art and had a gallery shop. I would like to have seen that."

"We did, and I miss it. Do I understand that your specialty is Southwestern art?"

"Yes, and I miss teaching about it. Here is an artist who is one of my favorites." He pointed to two of the watercolors and was describing their history when Jane reappeared with the tea tray.

"I was addicted to coffee in our teaching days," she said to Zora, as she arranged the cups. "But now Jamie and I drink tea most of the time. Very Canadian, I guess. Do you take anything in your tea?"

"Just lemon, thanks."

There was a short silence after Jane handed out the tea cups. Zora began to feel awkward. While she had readily agreed to accompany them home, she now wondered what they were going to talk about, other than the obvious: what Jane was going to do next. But it was Jane who, in her straight-forward manner, raised the subject.

"Ever since I've known that you were looking for me, I've wondered if this day would come. I - we - tried to stop that, as you know, but now you are here. Who else knows the truth at this point?"

"No one. I promise you. When I finally knew that Germaine had your picture by her bed, I did not tell anyone else, not even the detective in Columbus who has reopened your case. . First, I wanted to be sure I had found you. After that, I believe that what happens next is your decision."

Jamie intervened. "After your message came yesterday, while we were out at a gallery function, we stayed up a good part of the night. We talked about what Jane should do – what we should do." He turned to his wife with a look that Zora interpreted as both deference and love.

"I have more questions to ask," Jane said, "and I imagine you do, too. Maybe we can talk some more and then Jamie and I can tell you what we decided."

Zora nodded. She reached for a cracker and cheese. Suddenly, she was feeling hungry.

"You said you went to see Murray Parch. Do you think he has any idea that I am alive?"

"It didn't sound like it. In fact, it sounded like he has been thinking all this time about who may have murdered you! Obviously, if he could find that out, he might be able to get some exoneration and compensation for the time he served – just as you have considered."

"And Mai? Do you think she suspects the truth?"

"No, not at all. She certainly didn't say anything like that to me. She did seem very intelligent, though, but I had the feeling she still suspects Murray."

Jane stood up, taking the teach pot with her to warm up the tea. When she returned, she said,

"Your turn," sitting back down and looking directly at Zora.

"Well, I have wondered. I suppose this may be rude of me to ask, but did you have money hidden away somewhere? Hal said he found Social Security forms on your computer. But, of course, you couldn't have gone ahead with that once you became 'Evangeline'. And did you sell your jewelry?"

" After Murray swindled me, I opened a new brokerage account in mother's name. I wasn't able to put much away, but I did have some securities. Then, when I took early retirement from the school, I took a lump sum payment, with reduced annual payments for the future. Of course, I don't get those annual payments because I am 'dead', but I did invest the lump sum. So, when I changed identities twelve years ago, I had the means to live. And, conveniently, the secret account was already in the name of 'Evangeline McCall.' I didn't sell any of my jewelry. I gave some of it to the children's reading charity for an auction; I brought the most precious pieces with me here. Some are family heirlooms, and I could not bear to part with them. But I left a few pieces in my apartment, too, to make it look as if I had not planned to leave. I suppose Hal has those now."

Zora nodded.

Jamie reached over and touched Jane's hand briefly. "When Jane and I found each other again, I sold two paintings so we could afford this place. I didn't think my bachelor quarters offered Jane what she deserved. I still do a little consulting for the museum, and we have done well with our investments. Jane manages them. We have a comfortable life."

"I suppose if I became 'undead', I might be able to start collecting my annual school retirement payments, but that hasn't been an option. Until now."

Zora was surprised at Jane's last two words. "Does that mean you are thinking of coming back?"

"I might. That's what Jamie and I spent most of the night talking about. You see, it all hinges on Parch. If I thought he was going to die soon, it wouldn't make much difference if I resurfaced. But he's only sixty-six. He could live on for years. Of course, maybe the courts wouldn't do anything to partially pay him back, but we can't be sure." She paused. "And, to be frank, Zora, although you tell me you haven't let anyone know that you've found out about me, I can't be sure of that. So, I may get 'discovered' whether I want to or not."

Zora felt a flash of exasperation. This was certainly the old Jane – very firm, very sure of herself. "Well, you may or may not believe me, but since I only found out two days ago that you *might* be alive, I can assure you your secret is safe with me!"

"I believe that you *think* it is – and that you have done everything you can to make it safe. It's just that I don't trust many people. Perhaps that's a consequence of having been so badly deceived once. Anyway, I don't think I can reveal that I am alive until Murray is dead. And that may not happen before I pass on. If he should die, we've talked about at least visiting the U.S. Jamie is a Canadian citizen, and we've made our home here now. But I would like to see people like Phyllis and Hal."

Zora looked at her friend for a moment. She saw a woman very determined but calm in having made her decision. Jamie again took Jane's hand and held it for a few seconds. "We don't think we've committed any crime," he said firmly, "but I wouldn't want Jane to be exposed to any charges of deception or worse if we went back to the U.S." He paused and looked affectionately at his wife. "If we did go back – to visit – and Jane wanted to stay and it was safe to do so, well, we'd consider it. But we can't do it yet."

"Is there anything that would help you change your mind about at least letting people know you are alive?" Zora asked, trying to imagine how she would feel in Jane's place.

"I don't think so – not yet, at any rate. I know this is going to be difficult for you, Zora. People know you have been looking for me. What will you tell them?"

Zora had been wondering the same thing for almost twenty-four hours. "I need to think about that. Probably I will just have to say that my investigation has been unsuccessful. I don't want to cast any suspicion on Germaine, although the police may believe she was involved in your death. And the Columbus police are already planning to interview Murray again. Not that he can tell them anything. I'd like to let them know about you, but if I don't, they'll simply see Murray and not learn anything more than they have in the past."

They all remained silent for a moment. "If I - we - change our mind about this, I will call you right away," Jane said. "And it may be that I can reconcile 'coming back' even with Murray alive, but right now, I don't feel that I can."

Zora looked at her friend and inclined her head as if to say, "I agree." She felt sad now, knowing that people like Phyllis and Hal would never know the truth. "I will honor whatever decision you make – or make in the future, Jane. But may we stay in touch? I would hate to think I have come all this way to find you, only to lose you again!"

Jane got up and impulsively hugged her friend. "Of course, of course we will talk. Maybe the day will come when Jamie and I can even come to visit you. After all, no one is looking for 'Evangeline

McCall James' now." Jamie struggled to his feet to embrace Zora as well. "It would be a pleasure to see you here again, also," he said.

Zora felt that the meeting was at an end. She looked at her watch. "I was up at four this morning, and I'm fading fast. If you don't mind, I think I'll go back to my hotel and have an early night. I have a flight in the morning."

They accompanied her to the door. At the last minute, Jane said, "wait!" She disappeared into another room and came back with a book in her hand. "I want you to have this. This is the other 'Jane'. She has been my friend through many years, and I want her to be yours, too." Zora looked down. In Jane's outstretched hand was a bound, hard-cover version of Jane Austen's "Sense and Sensibility". Without warning, tears came to Zora's eyes. "Thank you," she said simply, taking the book. "I will treasure this."

They watched her leave. After the door closed, Jamie put his arms around Jane. "I think everything will be all right," he said softly. Jane kissed him. "Yes. Part of me wishes we could go back with her."

Zora walked the two blocks back to the park. There, she sat on a bench for awhile, thinking about the past two hours. She pulled her phone out of her pocket, immediately seeing a text message from Pete: "We are setting up our trip to see Parch. Call me later if you have anything new." She would call him, not telling him where she was, pretending she had been with friends. As she got up to walk the last four blocks back to her hotel, she thought "Now, I have the difficult part - making up a story about Jane Hubbard. But I'm too tired to do that tonight - I'll do it in the morning."

CHAPTER THIRTY

Ruth Elijah had a secret - two, really. She knew how to use the Internet, and she was keeping a scrapbook. Mrs. McKinley, the nice widow in apartment 202, had taught her how to get on line and Google. Ruth liked that word – she envisioned some friendly but invisible animal with large eyes living behind the keys when she pushed them. She knew other people like those people at NASA could use computers to do really important things, but for her it meant looking at pictures and stories in the news that she could understand. Once she had asked Mrs. McKinley to help her find her old minister, the one who had been so kind when her husband died.

"What is his name?" Mrs. McKinley asked.

"Reverend John."

"Does he have a last name?"

Ruth thought. "Yes, it is Knowlton."

"Do you know where he lived when you knew him?"

"Cincinnati."

Mrs. McKinley guessed at the spelling of his last name and went to her favorite "people finder" search site. Within a matter of two minutes, she had unearthed "John Knowlton", aged 84, still in Cincinnati.

"Can I write to him?"

"I don't see why not!" She copied the address for Ruth. "Do you want to write on the computer?"

This was even better! Back in high school, Ruth had learned how to type. She was a slow reader, and she had trouble putting her words together sometimes, but she did understand how to use a keyboard. With some help from Mrs. McKinley, she composed a short note to the Reverend Knowlton. Then, Mrs. McKinley let her print it on the small printer she kept on her desk. She even gave

Ruth an envelope and a stamp. In a week, John Knowlton had written back: "Dear Mrs. Elijah, I was so pleased to receive your note and know that you are well. I am in retirement here in Cincinnati and in good health. I remember you and your husband very well. He was a good man. May God be with you." Ruth read the letter over and over. She was thrilled.

After that, Mrs. McKinley suggested that Ruth could visit and use the computer any afternoon after 4 p.m. and before supper at St. Stephen's, which was at 6 p.m. Ruth didn't abuse this invitation - sometimes she skipped a whole week, but she did enjoy the times she could go on line. When her husband was dying and his eyes were failing, she used to read newspaper stories to him. She didn't think she was very good at it as she had to sound out the big words and read very slowly, but she had learned about many things and now would occasionally buy the *Columbus Dispatch* or *USA Today* from the vending stand in the lobby. She especially liked the pictures in *USA Today*. Gradually, over time, using the computer she looked up names of other people she had known in the past. Sometimes she found them. She didn't send any more letters but it was comforting to know they were there.

The scrapbook included pictures from her earlier life and more recent articles she had cut out from magazines that people left in the lobby or threw away. Sometimes, she saw something in the newspaper that she wanted to save. The scrapbook became several books, the earliest dating back some thirteen years.

It was now a rainy Monday afternoon. Her work for the day was finished. She was sitting in her room, thinking about Mrs. Erickson, the lady who had come to St. Stephen's looking for information about Miss Jane. Ruth had told Mrs. Erickson the truth about what she remembered of the last time she had seen Miss Jane. But she hadn't told that she knew more about the case because she had followed it in the newspapers and had cut out the stories about it. Then the stories stopped. No more mention of Miss Jane. Now, at least, someone was looking for her - or for her body -- again.

Ruth rummaged around in box on the floor of her closet. Here was the scrapbook with all those earlier stories. She read them again, slowly. That man, Murray Parch, had cheated Miss Jane. When she disappeared, that man was suspected of killing her. Later, he had gone to jail for the cheating. As far as Ruth could understand, the judge believed Parch had killed Jane Hubbard, although no one could prove it because they never found her body. Ruth knew that when you killed somebody, you usually went to prison for life - or at least for a long time. She had a cousin in Texas who was serving a life term for killing his wife. But a much shorter sentence was given to Murray Parch, although twenty years in prison seemed like a long time.

A thought occurred to Ruth. Was this Murray Parch still alive? Did he know someone was looking for Miss Jane? What if Mrs. Erickson found out where Miss Jane's body was? What if the person Ruth had seen with Miss Jane that last day was this Parch, dressed as a woman? Would the police arrest Murray Parch? Maybe that would make him afraid. Maybe he would be worried that he could be put a way for life. "And if he killed Miss Jane, he should be," Ruth said to herself. She did not like Murray Parch. Even if he did not kill Miss Jane, he cheated her. Somebody needed to tell him that the Black lady was going to find out what happened to Miss Jane. Maybe he would be so scared he would confess.

It took Ruth a long time to work all this out, but she liked the idea of scaring Murray Parch. "I could write him a letter," she thought, finally. In half an hour, she could go to Mrs. McKinley's room and use the computer. Mrs. McKinley usually made coffee when Ruth was there and watched her favorite afternoon TV program, something with lots of people talking. She did not bother Ruth but would help her if Ruth asked.

Ruth combed her hair and made sure she had her glasses. Then she went up to the second floor and knocked on the door to apartment 202.

"Come in, Ruth. Is there anything I can help you with today?" The TV was not on yet.

Ruth had rehearsed very carefully what she was going to say. "Yes. I need to find someone again. To write a letter to. I have his name." She gave Mrs. McKinley a slip of paper onto which she had carefully printed out Murray Parch's name.

Mrs. McKinley put on her reading glasses. "It's a rather unusual name. Do you know what state he lives in? That may help us find him." Ruth shook her head and looked down. She had not thought of this.

"Well, we'll get started and see what we can see!" Mrs. McKinley punched some keys and brought up the site she had used to find John Knowlton.

"Let's see. There probably few people with that last name. Do you know how old he would be?"

This was another question Ruth had not thought of. But she thought she remembered something from one of the newspaper articles of years ago. Did they say he was something like fifty? She knew Miss Jane had disappeared twelve years ago. She closed her eyes. With great effort, she did the math. "Maybe sixty two?"

In rapid succession, several names beginning with the letters "Parc" came up on the computer, but only four that went on to spell "Parch". One was listed as " Beverley", living in San Francisco. A second was "Kevin", in Oklahoma. A third listing was for "Mai", in Florida. Then there was a "Murray", living in Virginia. The site listed him as being 66. Ruth stared at the screen. She leaned over and pointed to the last listing. "That one," she said firmly. Mrs. McKinley nodded and copied out the address shown for Murray Parch in Winchester, Virginia, handing the paper to Ruth.

"If you don't mind, I'm going to watch my program now. Just call out if you need help with the computer." Ruth nodded, feeling both exhilarated and a little apprehensive now.

Thirty minutes later, Mrs. McKinley's printer spit out the letter to Murray Parch. It had taken Ruth several tries, but she was satisfied. The note was short:

"I know you killed Miss Jane Hubbard. I told somebody about it. I saw you in her car. The police know, too. They are looking for you and will come for you soon."

Ruth deliberated after printing the letter whether to sign it. She did not feel afraid of Murray Parch. "And it's not nice to send things to people when they don't know who sent them," she told herself. It did not occur to her that accusing someone of being a murderer was, perhaps, a more risky thing than staying anonymous.

She waited until the television was running a commercial. "I need an envelope, please, and a stamp," she said softly to Mrs. McKinley.

"Certainly, Ruth. Just a minute."

When Mrs. McKinley produced the requested materials, Ruth rummaged in her pocket and brought out seventy-five cents.

"Oh, no, dear, I don't need any money from you! I'm glad you enjoy using the computer."

Ruth felt embarrassed but placed the three quarters on Mrs. McKinley's desk. "Thank you," she said, taking the now sealed envelope and carefully placing a stamp on it. She would address it once she got back to her room.

"See you tomorrow?" Mrs. McKinley said gaily, as Ruth closed the door, but not before giving Mrs. McKinley a surprisingly big smile.

CHAPTER THIRTY-ONE

Since no one other than Jane and Paul James knew where Zora had been on Monday, it was easy to pretend she had been nowhere in particular. Her flight brought her back to Boston just after noon on Tuesday. As soon as she was able to turn on her cell phone, she saw that Pete had tried to call her. She found a quiet spot in the airport and called him back.

"I'm sorry - I had my phone off this morning. You called?"

"I did. Wanted to tell you that Carmine is flying out to Virginia Thursday to question Murray Parch again. He's asked me to go with him. Carmine thinks that finding Germaine's fingerprints in Jane's car and knowing her connection to Parch, it's enough to have Parch re-investigated."

"Will this be an official visit?"

"Not exactly. We're not telling him he's a suspect again, but we will let him know we're coming. If he wants a lawyer there, he can have one, of course. But we're hardly ready to charge him with anything at this point."

Zora took a deep breath. Was this the moment to tell Pete about Jane? It would save the Columbus police a trip and prevent unnecessary questioning of an ill man. But she couldn't do it. "Well, I hope the trip will be worthwhile," was all she could think of to say.

"So do I! But you sound dubious."

"Oh, I'm just doing sixteen things at once and not concentrating right now. I'm sure you and Carmine will be fine."

"If you don't hear from me tomorrow, I'll call you after we see Parch." There was a pause. "Be careful, Zora. I'll see you in a week."

After Zora took a taxi home and unpacked, she called Ellie.

"How are you feeling?" Zora asked, with concern.

"Really good, thanks. No more morning sickness. Trying not to eat everything I want, and that does *not* include strawberries, but, unfortunately, it does include chocolate covered peanuts!"

Zora laughed. "I'll look up some recipes for something wholesome but yummy and bake you a treat."

"Does this mean you will come to see us this week? We're here and I'd love to cook dinner for you, say, maybe Thursday or Friday?"

"Well, I'd love to, but I was really calling to invite you here next week, on Monday, to meet a friend who is coming into town from Columbus. I thought we could have drinks at my place and then maybe go somewhere pleasant in Cambridge. Maybe Italian? Roy may join us."

"Great! Is this a new friend or someone you knew in Dublin when you taught there?"

"He's a detective. The one who was in charge of Jane Hubbard's case. They've reopened it. Roy referred me to him and I met him when I went out there. We've been exchanging information since and he thinks maybe I can remember more if we talk in person, so he's coming here for a couple of days. He's very serious, but I think you'll like him."

Ellie tactfully bit back every question she had. How old is he? Is he tall, short, handsome? Does he have a sense of humor? Do you like him just as a professional acquaintance or as a 'friend'?" She didn't ask! What she did say was, "Let me check with Tyler, but I think that would be fine. Maybe you and I can have lunch anyway this week. I'll be at the university Thursday. Is that a good day for you? I can pick you up around noon."

"Thursday's fine." Zora hope Ellie would not ask the next question, but she did.

"How's the investigation coming?"

"Stalled, for now, I'm afraid. I'll fill you in when I see you."

On the plane ride home, Zora had made a check-list of the people she would need to bring up to date regarding her search for Jane. Obviously, she and Pete would see each other next week. In the meantime, she could wait for him to tell her about the upcoming meeting with Parch. Roy would not be home until Saturday, so no urgency there. Eventually, she would need to say something to Hal Hubbard. She felt more uncomfortable about Phyllis and even some guilt. How happy Phyllis would be to know the truth and how impossible it was to share that with her. With Ellie and Tyler, it was, in a way, easier. They had not known Jane. They would believe that Zora had exhausted all possible leads and believe that Jane's disappearance could never be solved. Zora reminded herself that Germaine had kept Jane's secret for almost thirteen years. "And now it's mine to keep."

* * *

For some reason known only to the gremlins at the Post Office, the "overnight delivery" registered letter from the Columbus, Ohio, Police Department, dated Monday morning, was not delivered to Murray Parch's assisted living facility, in Winchester, Virginia, until late on Wednesday afternoon. The front desk phoned Murray in his room, and he wheeled himself down to pick it up. He took it back to his room and read it.

In a way, he was not surprised. The Erickson woman was stirring things up. She had seen Germaine, and Murray himself did not know how - or if - Germaine had anything to do with Jane's murder. Of the fact that she *had* been murdered, he was sure. And maybe Germaine had done it? Their affair, lasting over two years, had been intense. And Germaine was a strong, passionate and, yes, jealous woman.

The letter from this Carmine Cisneros, Detective First Class, Columbus Police, did not give a reason for the upcoming visit, but clearly they had found out something – and he assumed he was again under investigation, maybe even suspicion, or soon would be.

The second letter, sent by regular mail from Chillicothe, Ohio, arrived Wednesday as well, but it got misplaced in the delivery boxes in the lobby. So, it was not until late Wednesday night that another resident – Mr. Chin – knocked on Murray's door to deliver it. "Got into my box by mistake. So sorry," he said, handing the letter to Murray, who looked at the post mark and did not recognize it. "Thanks," Murray said, closing the door.

Then he opened it and read it. He read it again. It was signed, but he had no idea who "Ruth Elijah" was. There was no return address. He had some dim memory of knowing something about Chillicothe, something from the past. Connected with Jane Hubbard? He did not know. But he now knew why the police were coming. Prison again in his future suddenly looked all but certain. Even though he was innocent of her death, could he prove it? He hadn't before. He still had no alibi for that day that would stand up in court. The woman he had seen that day was long dead. What if Germaine killed Jane? Would they assume he and Germaine were accomplices?

His whole chest jerked. He knew this feeling. His heart acting up again. He wheeled himself into the bathroom to get his pills. So many bottles on the shelf. Ten more years to live, if you're lucky, the heart specialist had told him. The pressure in his chest increased. Prison. Not somewhere he wanted ever to back to. His vision was blurring. What if he took all the pills now? All those bottles – and three more he had hoarded and hidden in the drawer by his bed. All of them together, maybe, would be enough. With his hand shaking, he filled a glass with water. His vision was getting worse, but he could see the labels on the bottles. One by one, he emptied them into his hand and took every pill in the cabinet. Then, he wheeled himself over to his bed and opened the drawer with the remaining three pill bottles. He struggled with one that wouldn't open, but he was able to take all the pills in the other two. He felt too weak to lift himself onto the bed. Maybe he would just stay here in his wheelchair for awhile to see what would happen. The room went dark, and he slumped over. Oblivion.

CHAPTER THIRTY-TWO

At noon on Thursday, just before Ellie picked her up, Zora got a text message from Pete. "Landed at Dulles. On our way to Winchester. Will message you later." Zora winced slightly. She could have prevented this visit to Parch, but now she was the keeper of Jane's secret. "Forever," she reminded herself. Would she eventually have to tell Pete? That thought had been haunting her, but she put it out of her head for now. "I'll know what to do when the right time comes," she told herself.

"I want to take you to a new Japanese restaurant in Wellesley Hills," Ellie said, as soon as she arrived. As the day was warm and beautiful, so they drove there and had lunch on a terrace overlooking a formal garden. They talked about the university, about Tyler's challenges in heading it, about Ellie's latest research, about the baby who would be coming in about six months, about Zora's family - everything except Jane Hubbard. Zora even shared a few tantalizing details about "Pete", whom Ellie was now very curious to meet.

At two o'clock, they started back to Cambridge. Zora invited Ellie in as she had made the sweet potato pies that everyone, including Ellie, liked so well. "Two of them, both for Tyler," Zora winked, as she wrapped them in waxed paper and tinfoil. As she was about to put the package in a large bag, her cell phone rang. Normally, politeness would have dictated that she ignore it, but she recognized Pete's number. "Excuse me," she said to Ellie, who walked into the living room and sat down with a magazine.

"Hello, Pete! I have company. Can you all me back a little later or can I call you?"

"Zora, Murray Parch is dead."

Zora abruptly sat down on a kitchen chair. "What, how, where are you?"

"We're in Winchester. A cleaning person found him in his room this morning. He apparently overdosed on pills sometime in the night. He may have been having another heart attack and tried to stop it. Either way, he's dead. No suicide note or anything. Carmine's dealing with the local authorities. There will probably be an autopsy." Pete sounded somber.

Zora tried to absorb this news, knowing she had to choose her next words carefully.

"Pete, I'm sorry the trip was for nothing. Maybe we can talk more when you get home. Are you going to fly back to Columbus tonight?"

"Yes, if I can get a flight. We were supposed to fly early tomorrow morning. I'll call you later. Will you still have company?"

"No. Ellie Sheppard and I just got home from lunch. I'll be here. Call me when you can."

She wanted to add something more comforting but the news opened so many possibilities that she couldn't quite put together another response to Pete. She sat holding the now silent phone for so long that Ellie poked her head into the kitchen. "Everything all right? I hope that wasn't bad news."

Zora looked at Ellie, her very good friend, her former neighbor, her role model for all this investigation. Suddenly, Zora started to laugh, a good deep down laugh, letting out so much tension, so much sadness. She got up, hugged Ellie hard, and said, "No, no bad news at all. Murray Parch has died."

Ellie stepped back and stared at Zora. "He's *died*? But you never proved he murdered Jane, did you? Why is this good news?"

Zora, touched Ellie's cheek fondly. "You'll see," she answered, still smiling. "Everything will be all right now, everything will come out."

Ellie stood her ground. "You have to tell me what you mean. You know something! You know who killed Jane. Tell me!!"

Zora led Ellie back into the living room. "I can't. Not now. But it's all right. If you can wait until next Monday night – I'm assuming you and Tyler can still come over for drinks and dinner – I'll tell you everything."

Zora realized that Ellie must be wondering if she had become unhinged. But Ellie gave Zora a quick hug back. "Fine. I'll wait, but you must know Tyler and I will be guessing!" She took the two pies, sniffing appreciatively. "And I'll probably eat most of both these pies in the meantime, worrying about you, and I'll get fat, and my gynecologist will get mad at me. It will be all your fault."

Zora handed Ellie her purse. "I hope so. That baby needs to start eating some *soul* food!"

After Ellie left, Zora made the call on her land line. She hoped someone would answer, and Paul did. "This is Paul James. May I help you?"

"Paul, this is Zora Erickson. I'm calling from Cambridge. I wanted to give you some news. I just heard from my friend, Detective Le Gall. Murray Parch died last night. I thought you and Jane would want to know."

There was a long pause at the other end of the line. Then, "I see. Jane is right here. May I put her on the other phone?"

Zora waited until she heard Jane's "hello?"

"Jane, it's me. Pete Le Gall just called. He and another detective went today to interview Murray Parch. Before they got there, someone at his apartment complex found him dead. The police think it was an overdose or his heart stopped. Either way, he's dead. He didn't leave any kind of note that they know of."

"Do they suspect foul play?"

Zora thought Jane sounded very calm, almost detached.
"Pete didn't say that. He did say the lead detective on the case would probably ask for an autopsy."

Zora thought she heard a short, whispered conversation at the other end of the line.

"Zora, let us call you back. Maybe later today? We need to talk about this."

"Of course, Jane. I understand. I'm here. You can call on this line or my cell. I don't think I'll be going to bed early tonight."

"Thank you. We'll call."

It was all Zora could do to not run out of her townhouse and down the stairs, jogging around the block and high-fiving complete strangers. Suddenly, she felt ten years younger. "Oh, Rashad," she said aloud, "I wish you were here to celebrate with me!" Instead, she cleaned up her kitchen, did a load of laundry, and then made herself a martini, using Rashad's excellent gin. She poured the drink into a plastic "to go" cup and left the house, walking briskly over to her favorite spot on the Charles River. Two crews were competing on the river. She decided to root for the ones in the blue-hulled scull. They won in a photo finish. "Some days, just about everything goes right," she thought. Draining her cup, she got up and started back home. Pete was going to call later, and also Jane and Paul. Zora looked forward to both conversations.

CHAPTER THIRTY-THREE

While Pete waited to board his plane at Port Columbus on the first Monday in August, he opened his daughter's email, sent early that morning. "So glad you are still working on the Hubbard case. What is this woman, Zora Erickson, like? Do you mind having to work with a civilian? Will you be doing much more travelling? Good luck in Boston. Call me when you can! Lots of love."

He debated about his answer for a few minutes. Then he began typing. "The case may be almost ready for us to close. Carmine and I are wrapping up loose ends. Zora's investigation started all this, and she gets the credit." He stopped typing. What else to say? Then, he added, "You would like Zora. She reminds me a little of you – and of your mother. Strong, like both of you. And, no, I don't mind working with her." He pressed "send" just as the boarding announcement blared out in the waiting area.

At 11:45 a.m., Zora Erickson opened the door of her townhouse in Cambridge and welcomed Peter Le Gall. At 11:46 a.m., with no warning at all, Pete Le Gall ignored her offered handshake and, instead, gave her a quick hug. Then he stepped back, looking a bit embarrassed, and looked at her. "Thanks for inviting me here." He stepped back a few paces. "This is nice," he said enthusiastically, after he had seen just the living room and the art she and Rashad had displayed. "Can I look around now or do you want to go to lunch?"

"I'll give you the tour," Zora said, wondering what Pete's bachelor pad looked like.

Pete commented on everything. He especially liked the kitchen, "now that I've learned to cook, I appreciate what you have here. My place is pretty small." He also commented on the brick and grass patio in the back, where Zora had a colorful deck table and chairs. "We could sit out here and talk," he suggested.

Zora suggested they have lunch nearby first at a chili and corn-bread place with an extensive beer menu. He liked that, too. She invited him to dinner, telling him Roy could join them along with "a couple of close friends". He looked a bit puzzled, but she did not explain.

Rather than discussing the case at lunch, they returned to Zora's patio to share their respective findings. Even though they had talked on the phone frequently over the last few days, they still had much to discuss. On the preceding Friday, when she talked with Jane and Paul, Zora had been given their permission to tell Pete their story. Now, he had his own news.

"We should get the results of Parch's autopsy today or tomorrow. Carmine will let me know. It doesn't really matter, but I'm betting it was a combination of a weak heart and the pills. Personally, I think it was suicide. He got Carmine's letter and later that same day, the letter from this Ruth Elijah. That may have sent him over the edge."

"Poor Mrs. Elijah," Zora offered, not for the first time. "In a way, she has been one of the most important people in the case."

Finally, at 3:30 p.m., Pete said, "I need to go back to my hotel, shower and change for dinner. What time are people coming?"

"I said 6 for drinks, then we'll go to dinner in Little Italy. I've made a reservation. With this crowd, everybody likes Italian food. Roy's coming, but Kressida, his wife, is staying home with the children. You'll meet her another time. You'll also meet Ellie and Tyler. They're at the university. Tyler is President. Ellie used to live next door to me. I helped her solve a case of murder once!" Pete looked taken aback, but all he said was, "You'll have to tell me about that some time."

"I'll be back here at 6, or a few minutes before," Pete told her, this time taking her hand in his and holding it for a minute. He had called for an Uber car, which came within minutes. Zora saw him out the door. After he left, she said to herself, "This is hopeless. I can't stop smiling!"

At 5:55 p.m, Pete returned. At 6, Roy arrived in his personal car. At 6:15, Ellie and Tyler rang the door bell. "Bad traffic!" Tyler apologized. Ellie was wearing a purple caftan that, Zora observed, that nicely disguised the newest member of the Sheppard family.

"Let's go out to the patio. Roy can play bar tender," Zora suggested. The ice bucket, glasses, bottles of red and white wine, Scotch and gin were already in place. Roy surveyed the table and chairs. Zora looked at him, amused. He was counting chairs – seven of them – and she had only told him about five people who would be there. She was certain he

felt embarrassed for his mother because she had made a small mistake: there were five of them here and she had set everything up for seven people. "Well, he probably thinks that age does catch up with us all," she said to herself.

Zora left the door from the patio to the house open. Even outside, she could hear the front door bell. Roy was just pouring the last of their drinks when the door chimes sounded. Ellie cast a questioning look at Zora. "Excuse me!" their hostess said. "I'll be right back. Probably FedEx."

When Zora came back down the steps, she was leading two people: an elderly, white-haired man leaning on a cane, and a smaller woman, very erect, smiling, wearing a brightly flowered dress and exquisitely crafted golden leather sandals. Zora came to the bottom of the steps and walked to the center of the patio. Her new guests paused, taking stock of the party. Roy loosened his grip on a wine glass he was filling and almost dropped it.

"Everybody, I'd like to introduce our new guests. They've come all the way here from Toronto to join us. Please welcome my new friend, Professor Paul James, and my very old and dear friend, his wife Evangeline, or as I knew her, Jane Hubbard."

Two townhouses down the block, the young couple who were renting there heard the applause, cheers and laughter from Zora's patio. "Someone celebrating something, the young man said to his wife, handing her a glass of champagne. It was her birthday, and they, too, were celebrating. "Yes, but they can't be as happy as us!" she said, toasting him and reaching up to give him a kiss.

However, seven people in Zora Erickson's back yard would have disagreed heartily with that last statement.